redemption

Chantal Chawaf

REDEMPTION

Translated by Monique F. Nagem

Dalkey Archive Press

Originally published by Éditions Flammarion
© 1989 by Éditions Flammarion
English translation © 1992 by Monique F. Nagem

Library of Congress Cataloging-in-Publication Data
Chawaf, Chantal.
  [Rédemption. English]
  Redemption : a novel / Chantal Chawaf ; translated by Monique F. Nagem.
  Translation of: Rédemption.
  I. Title.
PQ2663.H379R3813   1992   843'.914—dc20   92-511
ISBN: 1-56478-003-1

First edition, September 1992

Partially funded by grants from The Illinois Arts Council and the French Ministry of Culture.

Dalkey Archive Press
Fairchild Hall/ISU
Normal, IL 61761 USA

Printed on permanent/durable acid-free paper and bound in the United States of America.

redemption

1

As night fell, Charles became a vampire. He stared at the full moon. His figure was outlined like a black shrub against the high walls, and the shadows formed by his limbs and his trunk were moving over the rocky path that snaked its way toward hell. He has given up on the idea of kissing Esther, of holding her in his arms; he has given up on the idea of mingling his warm marrow with the shivering plant offering itself up to his mouth. Once again he tightly clenched his jaws on the resentment, on the bitterness. He is now ready to spit it back out, to throw it up. He chooses to wander, alone, in the darkness of the steep path from which he can only glimpse the distant lights of the frantic race toward the animated bedrooms still containing couples, the hope which he, this deeply wounded man, will never again experience in the slightest, even as an illusion. He has killed her.

Esther would have taken everything from him; she was ravenous.

He is at the breaking point. He is freeing himself from the clutches of the past. He aches, he suffers, but since that woman does not allow him to be human, then let him be inhuman! Let cruelty be his solace! May he no longer be the animal that she fastened to herself with their spittle, with their maceration, sticky, gluey, sickening like milk and yet so sweet, and he so enamored of the saltiness of her breasts, the warmth inside her skin. Oh! if only she would disintegrate in him, today and forever! If only there was nothing left in him of the one he loves, nothing left of this fusion and its heaven. Henceforth he would know nothing but the devil, evil, hate—all that prolongs indefinitely the torture of no longer being together, being bound, by lips and breath, one to the other, by the flesh.

Spirit of holiness, Spirit of light, Spirit of fire! Come kiss me, Spirit of joy! Turning away from her, will he understand the infinite mystery of the father's mercy, if the holy word enters his perverted and suffering heart, if he, the murderer, recognizes God, if the sacred word transfigures fasting, violence, and death? Ever since the murder, Our Lady of Silence has been watching over him, over his retreat. He can get ready, he has help, he is entering the kingdom, he is entering a state of meditation. He is touched by the Holy Spirit, by a passage from the homily that he is interpreting, adopting into his prayer, by this psalm on human misery, these sentences with which the Lord wants to shape his heart, although Charles resists the temptation with all his might. His fear is strong. He is changing, he is wary of this woman, of the other love. He is as pure as a priest; and out of obedience he goes toward the Hebraic poetry of twenty-five hundred, three thousand years ago, toward these psalms which triumph over the flesh, toward this reading which overwhelms him. There is nothing like the beauty of eternity, the deliverance which rids us of our sinful ways, which paralyzes the Holy Spirit; there is nothing like this thirst for the word of God which, alone, can overcome the bitterness of love. Then the man rises and the word becomes light. "Alleluia," the man thinks. His word becomes wisdom. Alleluia, his word becomes tenderness. Alleluia, his word becomes life. Alleluia. The word of the Lord is sharp, say the Scriptures. I saw that it was burning hot and sharp, the man whispers, and that it was cleansing me and I saw love flow out, depart from all my limbs and my being, and I triumphed over this beloved, hated woman; I ripped her open like a dog that gets run over on the road at night. I am finished.

I could no longer love her, no longer look at her, no longer sit next to her, no longer eat, no longer hold her close. I could no longer read, no longer write, no longer even drink a glass of water; I could taste my saliva, my tongue; I was smothering; I could remember her kisses; I was drained; I would get dizzy spells; I would hide alone deep under the covers of my bed and tell the image of this beloved and hated woman, hated because too beloved, "All I have left is your image and you are taking it away from me." And words came out of my mouth: "For me, to live would be to die." I realized that I no longer loved her, that I hated her. It was no longer her. It was no longer her body that oppressed me. Holy Jesus entered. You do not love Jesus for himself but for the comfort that he brings you. You no longer love this woman. You thought you loved her for herself but that was not true. "One must love the God of gifts more than the gift of God," said Saint Francis of Sales. One must love the God who gives more than what God gives. One must love God more than woman; the Lord taught me that from now on I will love him beyond this woman, beyond the unholy love of a man for a woman. Now it is you I love—praise be yours, Lord! Lord Eternal, your word is worthy, your word echoes in fraternal reunion. God of love, take me away from the other, from my flesh, from my penis, from my murder. Heal me of the beloved and hated woman— hated because so cherished—heal me of her. I implore you, the man convulsively whispers, eyes sparkling, teeth locked tight on the pain that is burning within him.

Charles was prowling through the ruins, through the rubble of his love for Esther. Those nights were very black, a little bewitched. Rage was driving him to climb the steep slope toward the fallen rocks from which he would contemplate the view of a disenchanted world, devastated by this blackness. An abyss of walls! A swarming of sadism! A haunt of impassable stones and bars. His own heart frightened him. He was imprisoned by relentless spite. Many lives, many reincarnations would not be enough to take revenge upon the one who had given him every-thing and taken everything back in the ferocious hand-to-hand combat during which Charles's senses had collapsed.

There was a full moon. The town's lights floated in an eerie fog resembling some alien galaxy. In spirit, Charles was traveling toward the celestial, ethereal ramparts, toward the lights emitted by the sky-scrapers, the stars, the airplanes and the satellites; in the black sky, they whirled around the hunted man, walled him in. He was set apart from the lives of others. He felt encircled inside himself, at the center of the earth, watched over by this faceless silence. High up on Europe's mountain, amid the ruins of the fortified castle and its chapel, he would jump at each sound he heard. He would listen to the barn owls, in the undergrowth, among ghosts.

In this secluded corner of the Alps, he was meditating on the mockery of love. For weeks he had been visiting sickbeds, tombs, pebbles, all that self-disintegration which aims for eternity, which soars only to come crashing back down. What is left of an ideal then? Cemeteries, archaeological sites, museums? Nothing living.

At the thought of Esther, he would become uneasy, he was unable to continue walking, he no longer had the strength to live without her. He missed her too much. He missed her sticky love, the rich, bluish foam of the sperm frothing inside the softness of the woman lying wide open and moist. "Bestiality," he concluded to himself. "Nothing but bestiality."

He walked through the vineyards, through the apricot orchards. The coolness of springs oozed out of the rock overlooking the valley. At night, Charles would stop at motels. He would pay for rooms he never even went into, unable to sleep between sheets, in beds which would have reminded him of pleasure since he was running away from his lost love. He did not think that he would ever feel alive again, that he would ever again meet someone he would desire as madly as this divinity. He had a harsh radiance. He was powerful, virile, muscular in his will to tear himself away from any trace of sensual pleasure. He was finally separated from her. He was man and no longer woman.

Charles de Roquemont continued to climb toward the peaks, trampling the crumbling ground where archaeologists were still excavating in search of perforated bones, parts of knolls, large gold crowns, pieces of pilings and shells from the days when this valley and these mountains belonged to the sea and the archaic kelp and green water civilizations. Charles was treading on this female potter, on the powder of the ages, on the layers of broken glass, of ceramic, the dust from the crushed pillars and tools, on the high mountain trail where the wanderer, still in love, still in a state of shock, was guided toward the late twenty-first-century sky, toward the beginning of the second millennium, hounded by the currents, by the dangers of absolute void.

At the foot of the mountains, the little village of Sion was bubbling and sparkling. The decomposing apricot-tree leaves released a carbonic gas into the late autumn, ruby red like a fruity wine. Charles took Rue du Tunnel, then Rue du Chanoine-Berchtold, then Rue des Fournaises to get to Tourbillons castle. He had with him a flask filled with melted snow. He also had his Bible and a Schwyzerdütsch dictionary he used to learn the medieval dialect, descended from Latin and German, which, long ago, was the only language used in the area. Having reached the top of the rock, Charles stopped to regain his breath. Then, addressing the clouds like a community of ghosts, elves, or fairies, he composed a poem that he bellowed in his guttural voice. He was worn out, exhausted with anguish. The towers, the fortresses, the stairs surrounded him. As night fell, he came back by Rue des Fournaises, by La Promenade des Pêcheurs, by Le Chemin du Calvaire, walked along the walls of Saint Francis House, followed the south wharf, pensively went down Rue du Vieux Collège again before returning, exhausted, to his hotel and ordering a beer.

He was losing weight, he looked emaciated. He decided, after a week of obsessions, to return to Montreux. He and Esther had spent a summer there, blue with sunshine. Once again he could see the mountains reflected in the high French windows that overlooked Lake Geneva. Esther, looking ghostly, facing the setting sun, had drunk hot chocolate, in the dark pink fading of the day.

In Montreux, Charles walked toward the Excelsior. He recognized the crystal chandeliers, the muted blues of the carpeting, the chairs, the sofas, the drapes. He went back to Vevey, to the Trois Couronnes Hotel. In the nineteenth century, Gogol and Tchaikovsky had stayed there. Esther and Charles had had tea there. He remembered those teas, those chocolates, those milks, those herbal teas, all those hot liquids which she drank, out of idleness, close to him as he silently adored her, as he ardently admired her eyes, her small, feminine hands. An hour later, she would get up, impatient. She would go to another tea shop. Charles, obediently, would follow Esther to avoid being separated, even for a moment, from his idol. She had turned him into a lady-in-waiting. But at night, oh at night, in their room, he would rediscover violence, he would leave this woman nothing of herself. There was nothing left in the softness of this pungent body that could resist him. "Where is the day, where is the night, where is my boy, no; my man, where is my man?" a song in the bar of the Trois Couronnes Hotel was asking. The day was waning, slowly, and out of this slowness modulating the twilight, Charles's memory was reborn. Everything that preceded the murder.

'2'

She is alone. The lamp is too close to her eyes. Olga Vassilieff thinks of sentences, words that are too hot, too true. One would need to reveal in detail what is hiding in her flesh, under her skin, in her bloodstream, to understand what is pulling the scriptwriter into this physical writing that she is working on so desperately. What will she bring forth? A script that will not be fit for filming. Sexuality, sensuality, viscera. . . . The round, full words are engulfed by the void of Olga's life. A director is paying her 250,000 francs to express what he has never guessed about love, and he will rewrite everything after her. Maybe Olga verbalizes what is impossible to film. Her script is an erupting, blood-red, rubbed-raw text. She should have been a novelist or a poet—not a scriptwriter, not the employee of a word/image factory. The flow of the body—that's too anatomical; those are not scenes for characters. What Olga would like to do is write from the flesh, from the veins, not fiction but excitement. From page to page, already, reality takes shape, sketches its almost obscene breath, the body gaining power over the spirit. It is not with a camera but with a scanner that these images of modernity could be placed into this intimate story, this suffocation which begins with the bursting need to name our longings, our instinct. "What's the matter with me?" she asks herself.

She stays up late every night. The script has to be finished by October. In the summer, Paris is quiet, people are at the beach. Olga is wasting away in the realm of a lost and vanished god, in whom she stubbornly insists on believing with an agonizing faith. Is the imaginary calling out to her? Olga, seated at her worktable, is drawn toward the other, this other she has yet to meet and who is never like the others, as though he were of a different nature from the all-too-human, too-limited, sinful men that she knows. Her heart, her nerves, her brain, her stomach demand something else from her, point to a creative outlet other than the script, other than Olga's literary gift for verbally re-creating life, for putting it into dialogue.

The radio is playing a slow song. A bite, a contraction, Olga is carried away by the impatient desire to meet someone, to dance to a melody modulating a mystery. An eye meets another eye; a mouth, another mouth; the skin, another skin. Suddenly you are two, one in the other. Held tight, one by the other. A cramp, deep inside her, keeps her continuously riveted to the hidden script, the one about the viscera on the alert, like holding one's breath during a moment of fear.

The wan rays of the moon penetrate her room, giving Olga the feeling that her body is making contact with the starry sky.

The next day around noon, as she wakes up, she once again feels herself turning into words, into sentences, into the script of this love story that she has two months to write. Night after night she creates dialogues that are nothing more than a monologue divided into two, three, four, a multitude of visions, illusions that are never defined, never acknowledged, obsessive fears of the flesh. No, she thinks, it is unusual to write the woman from so close up, to verbalize desire so strongly, to suggest with so much immodesty the intimate center of all this physical excitement. The movie will be rated X. And then it will be impossible to shoot. She is headed beyond the possibility of representation, where only the tangible, only the infinite sweetness of the physical like warmth, moistness, well-being, rumblings of desire can speak. Olga verbalizes the pre-verbal, the regressive. She gives speech to that which lacks it, such as hands, looks, lips, saliva, cheek, chest, caresses. She murmurs the moan of love and it becomes a language, a theater for the senses, verbal matter of the body, rhetoric of the mucous membranes, of mucus, of orgasm. She allows for the senses of smell and touch but not of sight. She pokes, she digs through live organs; she provokes them, there is no more fiction, there is only the story of a return to the most sensitive, the most sensual in us, to an orgasm. No actor, no actress, can serve as a go-between. No camera angle can possess the inner eloquence of the power of these words that bring us back to ourselves, with no detours, no metaphors. Here, we are inside what sighs, inside onomatopoeias. We are inside what is born of life.

Movies make everything visual. They're meant for the eye. But for this scriptwriter of the inner life, there is only the invisible, a long biological scene of life's gestation, a red, reddish, congestive imagination. The characters are not men or women but sex drives. The details, all heartbeats, ligaments, cells, corpuscles, get loose, separate, compose the bloodred symphony of the living body set to a music of whispers, liquid sounds, groans in its orifices, in the gaping feminine hole asking to be filled, fulfilled by God. Olga abandons her outlines; she breaks up the narrative, she squirts, she screams, she bathes, she wraps, she keeps warm, she squeezes; words become intertwined; there is a marriage with the verb *to love,* a wedding night in the allegory of the flesh. Olga does not tire of writing. She is tireless. Where is she? In which body? That of her mother tongue? She does not know anymore which one is working in her: the sex machine or the grammar machine. The abstract and the concrete fuse in the carnal inversion which, too feverish, too possessed, she is excreting. She can already hear her director shouting, "Cut the dialogue. It's too literary. You don't talk at times like this."

She gives speech to blood, to temperature, to heartbeat, to erection, to nipples, to clitoris, to penis, to the rubbing, to the arousal of licking; she makes life resonate over the whole surface of the skin and uses the sexual human body like a metaphor. She communicates; little by little, in her thoughts, she gives shape to a poetics of the body. From within her she releases the vitality of language and she subdues the rules of language which she uses only for sensitivity; she bends, folds, folds again, rolls up the linearity of the script which fits the curves of the flesh, the satiny smoothness of the skin, the loops of the innermost intestines, and her intimate writing resembles a fetus tucked away in the uterus, resembles the dilation of the cervix at the time of birth, and she writes the way a woman gives birth. Where is she going? Her joy at being able to create now, not with a dictionary but with life itself, leads the scriptwriter to what dead-end? To what impossible fiction? To what need for entwining the substance of words, for clinging as if to someone and for reaching the kernel, the heart of the sensitivity of words now rendered useless, become once more the flesh which verbalizes them, which screams, which torments, which pushes toward the other? By means of writing, of overflowing with writing, Olga falls just short of a certain kind of language, at the limits of some music, some mutism, some paralysis. As written language receives life, it also loses it, preserves nothing. It is a transfusion of last resort. The script might be saved but there is little hope of saving the script-writer. Olga Vassilieff, poet of effects, freezes, dies of writing in spite of her creative effort at reviving herself. Olga might not be intellectual enough, or maybe not happy enough. "I give up," she often tells herself. "Forget the contract, the 250,000 francs. I'll keep writing what I feel like writing. We'll see where it leads. . . . It will lead somewhere else. . . . I have to go somewhere else . . . to flee from here. I have to break down the barriers, all these words that divide, that confine, that isolate from life, which, the more they proclaim reconciliation, the more they betray it, the more they weave estrangement, the more they keep at a distance. I have to be straightforward. . . ."

She dreams of being free from the laws, the conventions of the script, of being emancipated from all writing techniques. Writing and filming are inadequate, rudimentary. But the director will get impatient:

"No, no. . . . We have to see them walk from the bedroom to the bathroom."

It is toward life that Olga is going and toward no other work. She feels distraught. She stops writing. Is she ready? Is it finally time to live?

Olga is walking outside. The summer haze rises, blue, above the grass. It is always possible to go farther. It is always tempting to go on, go down harder toward the fire, to venture deeper into the hearth. Walking in the park, Olga dreams of committing herself more fully to this vocation of life-giving words. Her other self, always suspect, always rebuffed, is taking shape outside of words. Olga suddenly needs more, much more. She can do more, as though inside her there were someone else, someone she needed to know better, that she would eventually meet, eventually bring out of herself to the light of day. On those evenings of vague melancholy, we have a premonition, we feel that there is a sister soul from somewhere else prowling near us, coming somewhere near us, who is going to complement us. It is not literature anymore. It is not movies anymore. It is here. . . . At the tip of our tongue, it is coming, it is becoming flesh.

Olga is back from the park. The words she begins to write again sprout eyes, a mouth, fingers which are on the brink of acquiring a real life through which the scriptwriter feels she is progressively being reconnected in her belly, in the palms of her hands, in all her heightened senses. But, because she has been seated at her worktable too long, she feels a cramp again. Olga braces herself. She hears the voice coming, a voice from her bowels calling her, emanating from her breasts, from their soft skin that no one fondles. Perspiring, she stops writing, she can no longer continue being interested in false characters who are separated from her flesh. Olga is shaking, too tense to concentrate on her page. Out of the blue she remembers an exhibit she attended the night before, where she was struck by an ominous photograph of Marilyn Monroe asleep, as if dead, in the back of a black limousine that appears to be carrying her like a coffin. Certain photographs, gifted with clairvoyance, make fate visible before it has manifested itself. Like the dreams that foretell what is going to happen to us, but in an incomprehensible language whose signs speak to us only later, when it is too late. Olga, increasingly tense, gets up, goes to the window, then returns to her worktable. Would the ghost of dead Marilyn agree to play a part in a script that would bring her back to life?

"I didn't want to agree to this exhibit," the photographer had confided to Olga at the opening. "I found these photographs of Marilyn too harsh. The poor thing has been so exploited. . . . So, one more exhibit!"

"This one is different," Olga answered angrily. "The photograph at Yankee Stadium is astonishing, or the one where Marilyn is at home, seated cross-legged. It's obvious from looking at your photographs that Marilyn Monroe symbolizes the body for those who are afraid of it, and she gives comfort because she consented to masquerade herself, to hate herself, until finally she killed herself. That's what's expected of her: to excite death. This relentlessness which this defenseless woman-child always inspires in her voyeurs is sadistic. We talk of desire but the myth of Marilyn is used to hide her admirers' impotence in the face of life."

Olga was almost shouting, she felt like clinging to the photograph. She wanted to delay her departure for home where once more she would find silence, solitude. She hated the artificial world of the movies that solved nothing.

Night after night, Olga is incapable of writing. Where to go? In what direction? She is about to lose her mind. Some nights anything, anyone would do to put an end to Olga's fast and her resistance to life; the different tempos of the sequence shots and of the long shots, the reaction shots that will film a mouth, a heart, a voice but not twenty-five lines, fifty lines of an overly polished dialogue; the words will be erased, useless, in the face of the intensity of a gesture or a look shot close up; the sound of the words will be shattered during mixing, at which time the picture and the sounds will intertwine in rhythms, beats, emotions. And from all that the scriptwriter has written, the director will keep only the sexual music of the flesh, and that will be rendered by the physical presence of the stars he will choose for the leading roles in the movie.

Olga feels frustrated. The window is wide open to the nocturnal breathing of plants and trees.

"I do not dare live. . . ."

3

It is a Friday evening. She has returned to the park. Something pernicious draws her there. At this hour, it is a little as if she were entering a garden of evil spells; the secret place of her demon, her bad habits. Something drove her back for a walk in the park, late, until closing time. She does not know what restless spirit forces her to neglect her work tonight, to neglect her discipline, her endurance, and to doubt herself, to walk about aimlessly, in the heat that precedes night.

"I really don't feel well; I should see a doctor."

The shadows become longer on the gravel path. A burning-hot breath of air stirs the parched shrubs.

"This is hell."

Olga spoke out loud. She did not notice that someone was following her. He was now ahead of her. He turned toward her and stared at her: "Hello!"

His light hair seems dark, as with some large spiders. Olga is dumbstruck: dusk hits her right in the chest. She is squinting. The light blinds her, as violent as a slap. The attraction is there, troubling, almost hostile. So he does exist. He burns you. He has a face, hair, shoulders, a torso, legs, a body, and above all, two fiery eyes that seem to reflect you as if you were seeing yourself through him. So finally one meets someone in a deserted park, in one's deserted life. . . .

He is man, she is woman. From each of these two bodies an animal attraction emanates. They are standing face to face; they look each other straight in the eye. Her heart beating wildly, she suffocates under the gaze of the other. She is embarrassed. Olga has the feeling that a strong wind has picked up, that it has sent her adrift through the park, where she cannot see the gates anymore, only the expanse of lawns and petrification; the statues look like large human seashells from another era. Olga and the stranger seem to have just sailed away. It is almost 8:00 P.M. The park is going to close. Olga and the man examine each other, nymphs, sylvans, fauns from a country which, from the duck pond to the frog pond, is born of the wind. They are getting ready, encircled by air; it is too late for contrary winds to prevent Olga from holding back the current which is throwing her against Pan. The satyr with the horns and feet of a goat has deserted the population of dryads, of hamadryads, of oreads, of orestiads, of napaeae, of limniads, of ephydriads, of potamides, of crenisae, of epigees, of all the nymphs of the park, the forests, the mountains, the caves, the groves, the marshes, the lakes, the rivers of night mythology which tinge Olga's eyes with sky and mist.

She tells the stranger that she is working on a script for a director: "I write words, words, words that someone else will turn into pictures. Everything will have a different meaning, it's demoralizing."

He scrutinizes her. "Meaning does not need words."

So says the god Pan. The slits of both eyes filter the moist twilight of summer. On the horizon, the oblique silhouettes outline wide surfaces whose edges, whose vague shapes form mirages of monumental proportions. Olga's sight becomes blurred. Olga feels herself being reflected in the other. She likes the leafy freshness of the park at this time of day. Olga and the stranger sit on a bench. She observes the man's nearly blond hair, which seems dark in the light of the setting sun. He speaks: "Over there, the West Mountain . . . The great dream for those who have nothing. The more we go toward the east, the more the images in our heads become bigger. In the neighborhood where I live, in the middle of July, everything is red in my street because of the geraniums and the roses. It looks like a field of blood."

He is near her. She is now inside someone. She is now outside of words, outside of work, waiting for something else. All that remains is to feel with her womanly receptor organs, with the sensuality of her skin. The man whispers, as rough as bark, as twisted as roots: Does she like nature? She does not answer. She listens attentively to this masculine voice, to its texture. The rustling of the utterances slides all over her body. She is brushed lightly, kissed. She examines the two virile lips, parted by the words, which must enable this man to swallow whole a woman bigger than he is. This manly mouth must reach its best during the fieriest part of the day or the night thanks to the mobility of the mandibular apparatus whose parts end in hooks, in words taking, promising pleasure. This virile tongue, long, thin, this cutaneous fold, forked like a dragon's tongue, must unfold, come brutally out of the barely opened mouth, and stretch out to capture, to shred, to lick female surfaces.

Olga will not need to stay up nights anymore, seated at her typewriter. Suddenly she is becoming unraveled, distorted, transfigured into the alchemy of a fantasy text where desire, instead of the mind, invents muscles, bones, a larynx, the feverishness of a real human being. A two-headed, bisexual androgyne conceived out of her and another, a chimera, enlarged, increased tenfold by the unlived life that this woman represses, abruptly sprung out of a chance meeting, on an evening of this beginning of the world when Olga, out for a walk in the park, projects suddenly onto this stranger too many dreams, too many impossible . . . What is his name? Olga questions the incarnation with the gigantic shadow: Eros, son of Venus and of Mars? Maybe we always move deeper into blindness, as though the nearer death approaches, the more urgently we are driven by the desire to flee from it.

`4`

Charles, before he even realizes what he is doing, makes Olga's smile disappear.

"I hate women . . . that's true."

On this summer's day which is not yet night, he remembers having known long ago this same woman standing before him on a summer's day when it is not yet night, when it is not yet dusk, and he remembers an entangled love and hate which, long ago, had devastated this same woman and himself, both bound to the history of their veins, of their organs, almost to the gestation of their existence, and he repeats: "I can't love."

She answers: "Me neither. . . . Maybe I can't; maybe I don't know how. . . ."

They stare at each other. He has light chestnut hair, yellowish blue eyes. "But I give pleasure . . .," he said.

Olga shudders.

The power of the body: who can ever avoid it? Or ever get over it after having experienced it?

"We're all afraid of the body."

Afraid to go too far from oneself, to be the other when the other takes you, puts you in him.

"Afraid to climax like a woman," the man whispers.

"To become nothing more than the penis that penetrates you, to be this man who . . .," the woman stammers.

"You can be pulverized sometimes; it can be so strong, you can be projected outside of yourself by such an inhuman force. . . ."

"You can lose your mind. . . ."

Then yes, all is possible. The colors are delirious. The seasons are inverted. Space expands as if there were no more walls and you lose yourself. . . . You lose yourself in the infinity of the other. Yes.

"You're no longer anyone."

She lets out a nervous laugh.

That his hair is a little greasy, that he does not look very neat does not much bother Olga Vassilieff. That he seems somewhat unbalanced, that he looks a little like a bum, like a drunkard or a failure does not worry her. He is handsome. A weird kind of beauty. He blew up the barrier of words inside Olga. He has spoken directly to her body and it is in her body that this speech is taking on meaning, gaining in size, unfolding; it is resonating inside her like the organ in a church, like sacred music, this music from the sacred life that Olga suddenly listens to with religious respect and almost with the fear of a divine law.

He takes on a serious tone to tell her: "I wish to see you again."

"Why?"

"I live in a studio. You will see my work. Nothing is put away. I just came back from a trip."

"You're a painter?"

"A massive project. A funereal dictionary. I bury definitions, meanings. No more language! Another language can be born!"

"Another language?"

"Silence. I detest the noise produced by words. I detest their cacophony. Why speak? When I speak, the sound of my voice prevents me from understanding what I say."

She watches him.

"I tear pages out of a dictionary and with scapel and awl I perforrate: I cut the letters away from the words. I gash the syllables. I split up citations into twos, threes. I slash meaning. I glue each sound separately on a little piece of cardboard that I pierce with pins or toothpicks and I stick the word on a stand. Nothing is recognizable anymore. The entire language loses its function; it doesn't communicate anymore, it doesn't have meaning anymore. Nothing circulates through the words anymore. They're dead. Language stands around like candles lighting a corpse lying in its coffin. It's no longer a reclining woman, receptive to the man who embraces her and gives her life."

Olga shivers. "It must be interesting," she forces herself to say.

"I hope that one day the dictionary becomes a deserted space, a box that opens and from which words fly away, the way children leave their parents' house to lead their own lives. I hated grammar at school. And one day, I decided to settle the score with this dictionary, this prison, once and for all. I began by throwing the library's big dictionary out the window; then I went downstairs to pick up the remains. I picked out the guts (the pages that had become unstitched, unglued); I took away the contents that were scattered on the ground and I listed everything in order of hatred. The words I hated the most, I placed them at the beginning of my list."

"Which words? Women? Other men?"

"*Mother, penis, belly, sex, to love.* . . . Those damned, sickening words that serve as a pretext for all sorts of hypocrisy and pretense. Feelings are hateful, whether they are filial, maternal, paternal, sexual; love is a jumble of disgusting orgasms that should not be acknowledged. We never worry about the one we think we are worrying about. What we are most obsessed with is a thought, an unhealthy thought that we try to hide. The devil is somewhere: our private devil makes us betray those we come near. And we betray them with what? With speech, with words, and what we call charity is nothing more than pure sadism. Exchanges between individuals who think they are speaking to each other are nothing more than delusion, deception, calculations, manipulations, ravings. . . . So, to do away with language, to keep only nouns, which are no longer symbols but just matter, just letters, is to preserve life. Let's do away with wholeness, leave us only with parts. Let's have everything disintegrate: bold type, capital letters, small letters, downstrokes, upstrokes, and then these lousy words will no longer represent anything, communicate anything, and the racket will stop, language will only be space, and we'll be able to breathe, we'll be able to travel through it instead of being stuck in it. Language should be nothing more than an image, nothing more than a beautiful image with no context around which we can dream of images of the image; the words should be shapes only, so they can't identify anything anymore. We don't need to understand. We only need to let ourselves be carried away in a language which must be solely that of our body, our skin, our flesh, toward the infinite dream. The air we breathe, the blood which circulates should no longer hold us back on earth; let's fly away, and language will be no more than signs which refer to nothing other than the mystery of boundless space, pure imagination."

Olga stares at the mad dreamer. These words departing for destinations unknown set her free. And once rid of words, where are we? She is slowly getting dizzy. Will the words of her film script leave their prison to live out their freedom? The scriptwriter now wants to write only free, madly free life. Olga wants to externalize herself, to go outside herself, to go toward the other even if, like this man who is probably sick, she has to lacerate a dictionary with a knife the way a matricide would lacerate with a razor blade the face, the breasts, the vagina of his mother in order to come out of himself, to extricate himself from the inner world which holds us all prisoner, as if we had never been born, and prevents us from reaching the outer world.

"We say *mother tongue,*" thinks Olga out loud.

"For me, language is just a body, nothing more than a miserable body that we finger, that we kiss, that we lick, that we prick . . .," the fanatic whispers. Olga, deep in imagining, analyzes nothing. She experiences. She listens, lets herself be rocked, infiltrated, destroyed, segmented by the barbarian, by the raving mad poet. She too wants to go where there are no more words. She follows the progress of the insane mental scaffolding; she penetrates the desecration of this dictionary, which has been dismembered, dislocated, disjointed like a woman's body: the maniac, leaning over the lips of his dying mother, would have desperately tried, by defiling her, to violate, to corrupt the secret of life.

"I frame the cardboards where I engrave the pieces of syllables in black. The remains . . . it's my setup. I'd like to show it to you."

Olga, obsessed, regresses; there will be no more words, no more speech, no more writing, only that part of the body, the uterus, the vagina, the hole filled by the penis carving into the flesh, into organic life. There will not be a need for symbols anymore; meaning will disintegrate and reveal once more only matter, only enjoyment, only pain, this prelinguistic dough, orgy, this life which Olga can feel flowing out of her intestines, which are more twisted than ever by privation.

Time will become inverted, she believes. This mental deficient will show her the way. She will go back in time when there was no language yet to express oneself, when we were not yet capable of thought, only of feeling. There will be no more words, no more anything. We will only be able to suffer and cause suffering, and to rejoice, yes, without any restraints whatsoever. She will no longer repress her feelings.

"Words are all similar, like road signs," says Charles. "It's our heart that gives them life. Otherwise a word is nothing. I want to paint words red, like the heart. And then let them live like a body, so we can look at them, touch them. I have taken that impersonal thing called the dictionary and have tried to make a human out of it, with eyes, a heart, hands, to give life to words by releasing them from their closed box; by planting them in the open air, I have tried to animate them with my own life, my own fatigue, with my work, to hold them in my hands, to clip them, to cut them up. My eyes go blind after twelve hours a day spent on them, looking at them painstakingly with a magnifying glass and reducing them to fragments, to letters, to syllables like musical notes, sounds, cries. The whole word isn't necessary. It's enough that the sounds make music, the rest can die. . . . All the rest."

They look at each other; they understand each other. Charles de Roquemont seems exhausted.

"It's not the meaning that matters. It's harmony. It's feeling good, it's not being harmed by words, no longer suffering, as when we speak to each other, when we say dreadful things to each other, when we tear each other apart, when we could kill each other. So I give words wings, the wings of a fly. They're tiny and black like flies and I help them fly off. Words are insects. Like the living, they need air, light, rain. At my house, where they're glued to the wooden pins, outside of the book box, they're happy, they live out their lives. I'm going to exhibit them in a museum."

Olga, perplexed, scrutinizes the man. "What's it like to spend eleven hours a day on a wrecking job, over paper dust, ink, glue, breathing culture in bits and pieces? Is it really exciting for you?"

"No. But artists are like heroes. They must show others the way."

"You think your job is heroic?"

"Yes."

She senses a megalomaniac. She could just as well sense a Jack the Ripper in this language-slayer. Seduced by his pathology, Olga listens. He is explaining how he manages to prevent language from representing, communicating. Language must not communicate anything. That way the beauty of what lies beyond words, the narration of self-extinction, the journey into the unspeakable, the myth of sweat, of sperm, of tears, of contraction, of pain and of desire that make up the world of our tortured bodies, can come to light.

For two hours, Olga, fascinated, has been listening to the stranger. The park is going to close. It is almost night. Olga is dreaming of someone who would know how to write upon the flesh. This man?

"That does not change the dictionary. I wanted to shake it up. It was provoking me. I had fits of anger: I was going to drain all of its words, I was going to throw them all on the floor! They were going to be quiet! There wouldn't be this noise in my head as there had been before . . . this infernal buzzing that I couldn't stop, that even automatic writing couldn't help me in transcribing . . . it would go too fast . . . it would bang too hard in my brain . . . in my blood . . . I would have needed a machine behind my forehead to record how fast this was all rushing through my mind . . . it was going too fast . . . I couldn't think."

Olga in a distracted voice asks, "As if you were inside someone who prevented you from leaving?"

"Yes. It has to be straight, rigid in order to rise high, in order to make a hole in meaning. So that meaning will not possess us anymore, will not tell us its truths and its lies anymore. We just need to touch with our hands, with our fingers, we don't need the mind if we have the heart. For five years I've been making holes, perforating in order to demolish these damned barriers, so there will no longer be these words which always take me away. . . . Always more . . . I want to go beyond solitude, you understand? I want to give life, love a chance . . . I want to be able to go toward the other."

"Me?"

"I don't want to feel paralyzed anymore. Words will say anything. When we can touch, we are free from loss," he screams. "To touch with our whole hand, all our fingers, our whole skin, with our sweat, with our work. We must be able to touch words. Words have nothing to do with the oral, it's the visual, the tactile, the sensual, that's where we perspire, where the image separates from reality and where, unreal, it's even more fascinating than a mirage when we are feverish and think we are fondling, kneading the impossible, an impossible woman . . ."

Olga Vassilieff, seated in Monceau Park on this summer evening, is listening to Charles unburden himself:

"The word is beautiful when it resembles a bird soaring up in the skies or a fighter plane surveying territory. That's when the word is beautiful. When you don't have a name anymore, when what you've done doesn't have meaning anymore. When it's only something ephemeral, intermittent like the sensation of being submerged in space. All we have to do is hang on, grab on to avoid falling back into the void as if we were frantically knocking against the obstacle so it'll open the door for us, so it'll let us come in, howl, cry in anger as if we wanted to force the words to listen to us, to take us, to make room for us, to give us their place, as if we wanted to be in the place of words. Force her to take us in her arms . . . to be closer . . . closer to her . . . to be in her . . . adhere to her, to her breath . . . to cut off her breath . . . to find her again . . . to love her!"

He is yelling. Olga is under the spell cast by those two beautiful, mad eyes. Her stranger will not let go now. He clings to her as if he were drunk.

"This damned language, this bitch, this damned slut who always refuses to put out. . . . She'll give herself only to take herself back. We have to slit her throat, drink her blood, eat her guts. Go to the quick of her ardor, of that part of herself she's always refused to surrender, the slut. We must force her to give up her soul, put pressure on her, get her hot, screw her, nail this tart, melt this ice cube, this whore, so she'll have a jolt before croaking!"

Olga, stunned, is looking into the shadows. He continues:

"This shitty bitch! This dirty bitch for whom those damned sons of bitches jerk off while waiting to hang themselves after having gotten even with her!"

"Have you lost hope of ever making yourself heard?"

"Now I depend on nobody; I'm independent. . . . Eleven, twelve hours of work a day . . . with my knife and two dictionaries for the front and the back of the page. I'm like a copyist. This whole work, the dictionary, I'm redoing it, I'm writing a new type of manuscript: with holes, with perforations. It can be seen but it can't be read. It's simply beautiful."

He pauses, assesses the impression he is producing in the astounded eyes of Olga, and continues, more calmly:

"I want to prove that words are objects. It's up to us to subject them to our will, up to us—not language—to lay down the law."

The woman feels intimidated by the growing power this madness is having over her consciousness.

"When I work, it's as if I were a machine. I have hallucinations. I see space, only space, a limitless desert. All those words, all those pages are long . . . more than two thousand. To count the number of words . . . to retranscribe everything . . . subtracting, omitting. To impose a void, silence on what has been full and noisy for the more than two thousand years since our language was formed. Patience, discipline are necessary to tear to pieces, to shred this monument. After a hundred words, I get tired, my eyes hurt. The bulb in my lamp is too bright. It gives me headaches. My back is broken from bending over the words. I'm a strange kind of writer. A failed, impotent writer, if you wish. Unlike you. . . ."

"Failed, certainly not. You seem more like a creator. Maybe a little murderous."

He turned pale.

That a man could grow freely in the thoughts of this woman is what matters to Olga. The evolution, the development of a shadow, the tentacles of this shadow, the gigantic proportions of this parasitic shadow. It is the shadow he projects that moves Olga; it is this shadow that she will, with all her heart, extend to the city, to the bars where they will meet, to the rooms where they will love each other, to the avenues, to the traffic, to the soft lights, to the elevators, to the smoky darkness of a discotheque, to the velvety interior of a taxi silently, steadily driving through the night, to the weekends by the sea or at the mountains, to pleasurable settings even more than to pleasure. Olga is functional enough to transform her script into this halo encircling the moment, the disquieting seductiveness of this man whose name she still does not know.

"Where's your studio?"

"When I'm asked this question, I feel like answering: nowhere. Because often, at home, I don't feel comfortable, a little as if I were a stranger in my own body, in my own language. Yes, I live in emptiness the way a loser always ends up stumbling into unfilfilled dreams. I would situate my territory in obliteration, in retreat, in estrangement, in oblivion, as opposed to the fury which I also inhabit at other times. What's your name?"

"Olga."

"Can you imagine what it's like to be dispossessed, to be cast out of reality all those days, hours, nights? Sometimes I have had enough of violence. At night I collapse on my bed, my body exhausted from the feat of dislodging words, language, of dragging them into permanent instability, into total constraint. It's so exacting. Imagine the feat of strength that an artist requires of himself when, instead of silencing himself, he decides to silence the whole language, the entire lexicon. Do you realize the scope of the project? And the difficulties in bringing it to fruition? I've lost all feeling, I'm like a telex. To repudiate, repudiate, repudiate, repudiate. Isn't art perverted? To pass off the act of killing as the act of creating?"

He questions her with his eyes as if he were imploring her. She can't follow him anymore. He is slipping. Is he referring to himself? She is afraid. She detects traces of sadism, madness, or genius in him. Something in this man never matured. He continues:

"Amid general apathy, who blames whom for the destruction? They don't even notice that they're in the process of blowing up everything. So, naturally, I participate in the universal explosion. What else is there to do? And anyway, they couldn't care less that their language is going to pot, not one bit! I feel no guilt whatsoever."

She jumps. He insisted on the word *guilt*. This man is heading in the opposite direction. She will catch up with him. She will put him back on the path to innocence. There is a tremendous force in Olga that dreams of conveying to a man the life toward which the words of her own script are no longer the true route. . . . Olga experiences a desire to nurture. Perhaps this one who is in despair, in need, oh yes, she is ready to give and keep on giving life's spirit.

He moves her to pity. He interests her. They have recognized each other. Even if he is raving, even if it is worse.

"I'll make a wall mounting with what's left in print, after I've finished cutting. I've kept the margins, the paragraph indentations. Cutting every day is long and tedious. It's monotonous work. But I want to persevere, question time, craft. . . . It's not meaning that interests me, it's appearance. And if I must suffer to do this work, then all the better. To test oneself builds character. One becomes a man. . . . I picture words as if they were districts or neighborhoods . . . the boulevard of verbs . . . all the verbs are red. The adjectives are freeways, yellow like the sky I used to see far away in the town where I got the idea for my project: Artabassa. I won't tell you where Artabassa is. It stirs up too many memories for me. . . ."

The day is waning. The colors of the park sail away toward Olga knows not what dream of escape to some eternal childhood, to the land of eternal freshness where the grass is eternally beaded with dew, the flowers never wilt, all year long the forests preserve the scent of the violets hidden in the foliage whose leaves never fall. There are no tentacular cities to choke the wind, the sky, chests; there are no mentally ill, love is not restrained. Life within us bursts in a shower of sweet pleasures.

"As on a pleasant walk," continues Charles, "you're walking through hoping to learn. At the word *dart* you go to the *d*'s. I was fed up with distress, with this perpetual conflict. With having to fetch the words, fight against them. . . . Now, it's going smoothly . . . I'm breaking through. I have support. My perforated pages will be hung in the greatest museums. Yet, it'll be my own passage. The tale of my journey through language."

Where does this inner zeal come from for slicing into spirit and turning this spirit into an animal that one disembowels with mad delight? Olga is intuitively on the alert. Risk damnation! she swears, yet discover, even fleetingly, savagery! Defy the cruelty of life and death. She is ready to dive in, to descend into the deep waters, deep in the heart of night.

'5'

Just what is madness? To love in vain because only to hate is possible? To shake a woman until she moans because she seems too docile? To shake her 840 times and, with the spasms of her body, her organs, her bowels, produce a happening of sex and death. To exhibit the still-beating heart of this woman, to rummage through her intestines, to make a spectacle of the disembowelment and, like some rock singer, give a concert with the cries of delight she lets out, unaware that she is being killed? The mad labor of her streaming blood, the madness of an artist of woman's agony, of sinking into an orgy of blood. The madness of a man saying of this woman that he will kill: "She will be me. Thus I won't have to love her, to desire her, to risk being abandoned by her anymore . . . she won't frighten me anymore." Madness . . . madness, the woman, blinded, is ready to lock herself up in a cage with a coyote for a week. She is ready to allow the mad musician to play 874 times the same deafening song on the keyboard of her nerves. He holds a stopwatch for four minutes and he imposes silence on the female instrument screaming with pain: "Restrain yourself," he says as he is eating her breasts and her vulva. "Restrain yourself from suffering for four minutes . . . listen to silence approaching like death. . . ." And for fourteen hours, not drinking, not eating anything other than this woman, he drains her of all her breath while she is burning with desire. But what else can a man without an erection do but be mad or drive to madness? Mad with power, mad with impotence? To ask a doctor: "Can I?" Answer from the doctor: "Don't love her, don't touch her, thus you can guard against any surge of excitement in you." What to do about the impotence of desire? Other than, yes, become mad, drive her mad. The man examines this stranger, Olga, whom he thinks he recognizes. She reminds him of the other, the one who had driven him to the doors of the psychiatric hospital, to drink, to get drunk during hellish nights, to sob, to deaden himself, to try fanatically to forget her in the frenzied ravings of his deranged mind. The stranger's eyes survey this somber man. His hair is coarse, curly, chestnut, almost blond. His shoulders are very wide. His back is straight, his hips narrow, his stomach flat. His tall and limber figure is naturally elegant and the paleness of his yellowish blue eyes seems to probe sadly into eternity, the kind that represents an absence, an unbearable lack.

Just what is madness? Fourteen hours, seventeen hours, nineteen hours of obsessions and lunacies a day. . . . It is accumulation . . . mad accumulation . . . it is eating human flesh until indigestion sets in; it is feeding on the life of the other . . . to be at once nauseated and ecstatic . . . to have a full mouth, a full mouth like a vampire. To want the townspeople saying: "The vampire has struck the 450th time. . . . It's the 450th time that he chews, that he swallows the soft, pulpy flesh of the hemorrhaging woman lying on his bed." To have delusions of grandeur, the grandeur of the carnivore so the townspeople will go along with your act, with your anthropophagy: "Sir, what's the idea of constantly playing this morbid melody? What symphony of horror are you composing? Don't you respect the body?" The vampire proudly answers: "I'm uncompromising. I'm a maniac, a fanatic. I don't want to pause. It's a funereal art. The odors, the perceptions, the sensory level must continuously rise, spread death's rapture through the town." The town is like an arena where the beast spars with his brain for five hours, six hours. The act becomes automatic; we are a machine, we start to play again, we are not able to stop. The problem is to count the 848 times when all notion of time has been abolished . . . to devour without throwing up 848 times. To suck 848 times. To integrate without vomiting. Not urinate, not defecate. One hour . . . Seven hours . . . Who knows? We chew noisily, gluttonously. Not that there is much fondness for the sporting side of this, for the marathon of breaking bones, ripping skin; the gums, the teeth, the hands, the fingers that do the dismembering during the act of love, during the tireless eroticism of the sucking and the licking, get tired. . . . There was still one more round . . . two more rounds. . . . It was necessary to continue, playing on this piano of vertebrae, of ligaments, of orifices, of mucus. . . . How to remain anonymous? The whole town will talk about you. . . . You have succeeded in loving without being answerable. . . . It lasted nineteen hours. It was total happiness. . . . It was you, alone. You were inside her as if you were alone. You no longer felt any human presence. . . . You were alone in your room as if the body of this woman were not lying underneath you. And she no longer begged you to love her and the concert-hall acoustics of the bedroom would let you hear, amplified, the beating of her panting heart but inside you, there was nothing human . . . no rushes of affection toward her . . . no compassion. . . . You simply needed to see her suffer, to make her suffer, to reduce her to impotence, this cursed impotence which you had to exorcise. You had to make this woman impotent in your place . . . you had to kill her. To kill love, desire, because you are this impotent man you detest. He watched the victim raise her tear-stained eyes toward him. It was in Artabassa. That night the whole town was fantasizing, was identifying with him, the madman thought, that night he and his crime had the support of all the people. It was a

night of bloody ritual when the artist was performing death at this concert which would last seventeen hours. Seventeen hours of butchery.
It was as if he had wanted all the people around him to say in the night:
there's someone in town who's making love. The concert artist has
arrived at the 450th time; the lover has taken his mistress 450 times
since dawn. And the townspeople, surrounding the night of love, surrounding the eventual death of a divinely erotic woman, were waiting
for the vampire's exhaustion. However, nothing in him was weakening, neither his vision nor his hearing. He kept up the rhythm. The
electrical discharges going through his head were not disturbing him;
on the contrary he felt his energy double; he had the sensation of
having two penises, two anuses; he was ejaculating endlessly; his
sexuality was becoming mechanical; never again would he make love
this way, with such a breathless panting which sounded like atonal
music. After each orgasm, he tasted blood and cognac; he felt like
having another sip; he counted the veins, the capillary vessels on the
fleshy mass which the room's air-conditioning and fluorescent light
were beginning to alter. Before this corpse, he was left with no
emotions; he sniffed her; he sensed a barrier. He could not go on
anymore. His penis was a knife. He slashed her. He wanted to enter
her from all sides, take possession of her hips, her belly, her kidneys;
he wanted to plant himself in her; it was matter, it was alive and if he
were to step in it, he could break everything; he had to be careful, to
restrain himself, to calm down; it was better not to ejaculate all at
once. It could take two hours, three hours of control to prolong the
intense pleasure of feeling her die little by little. . . . He was panting,
exhausted, but he was not giving up; he would do his best to defeat her.
What is madness? Straight streets lined with identical houses like
rows of factories whose machines operate night and day and whose
mad, rumbling turbines spit smoke out of enormous furnaces inscrib-
ing onto the sky, as on a screen, snatches of words so enlarged they are
nothing more than their own materiality, nothing more than disconnected feelings amid the letters of some gigantic alphabet forged by
the hallucinations that haunt, splitting the days and the nights in the
disintegration of the world, in this battle which a sick man is waging
against his own body; it is blocks of dense rage, it is black cubes; it is
menacing masses; it is petrification; it is the *e*'s, the *s*'s, the *t*'s, the *h*'s,
the *e*'s, the *r*'s of a first name: Esther. It is teeth turned into a saw. It is
the dental ivory of a kiss. It is lips almost turned to mineral. His
tongue, his teeth poke into Esther's flesh, into the hollow of Esther's
motionless hand grasping onto fistfuls of nothingness. . . . It is the fall
of the whole weight of desire doomed to collapse as soon as there
are dreams of existing in the other's starry eyes where we cannot go

anymore, where we do not proceed toward the other because then all we can be is the other, not ourselves anymore; we have lost our way if we go where we persist to cut, to slash, to bite, to tear, to be utterly envious. . . . What is the proof of madness? To feel one's own body as limp as a plastic garbage bag full of trash, of dead fetuses, of vomited beer and wine, of dried sperm; it is the incessant buzzing of language that must be silenced like this woman whose obscene hole must be plugged, to finally escape from it, to be free of it, no longer speak the same language. . . . It is ripping off skin, flesh. It is splitting oneself in two. The other young woman, sitting on a park bench in the summer night, continues to look at the stranger who appears more to be dreaming her than seeing her. She asks: "What are you thinking about?"

He mumbles, startled, "A woman. . . ."

"What woman?"

"It could be you."

His large shoulders are stooped. He leans toward the ground as though he were about to collapse.

"You don't feel well?"

He straightens up, takes in a whiff of air as though he had difficulty breathing. He does not answer.

"Do you exhibit often?"

Artabassa. A name in the mad snow, in the resonant swirls. Artabassa, like an inhuman roar, like the whole dehumanization of the world, the whole impotence of a monster admitting his monstrousness. Only the stars in this woman's eyes had signaled to him far away, up north, in the snow, signaled that she would be willing to lose her name, to have it merge with the name of this town, Artabassa, a place devoid of meaning; the man's memory was fading. He had been mad, an embryo of a man who could not manage to be born, and sadism had taken hold of him again; he had his fury and since then, to atone for it, he removed the stars, removed the sky, and obsessively, each night, put them back in the eyes of this woman whose look of horror he could not forget. What is madness? It is this woman with the starry eyes, this shiny music; you want to love on another earth than this earth, as if there were two earths. And if the second earth, over there, beyond the freeway which was an extension of the boulevard, beyond the first earth's horizon, would part open under the light emitted by the illusion which beckoned you to Artabassa, would give you a second chance to come into the world, would promise you these regions of the ends of the earth, whose color, at the extreme northern part, would not be those of oceans and continents but that of placenta, the biological red where you could go back into the uterus, dismantle this man that you do not know how to be and, in the inner darkness, remake him as a woman, as if you could rejoin your first hours, your first weeks, the moment of origin when any man is female, does not have a masculine sex yet, does not yet belong to any gender which will differentiate him from the female and her belly where he is still part of the whole. What is this madness when a woman, all starry-eyed, charms you and nabs you with a promise to give you back your life? What are love's lies, these lines which twist, veer, change shape? What do you call having been weak enough to believe her and to give yourself over to her and to rush into her deep embrace? At Artabassa, five years earlier, in a New World skyscraper, on the twentieth floor of a hotel made of steel and glass, Charles had loved Esther all night long and, at dawn, surrounded by sky, he had made a hole in her belly and let himself out.

"You're crying?"

He is crying his heart out.

"It's nothing. I drank too much."

Esther, over there, had never been so beautiful as on this night which, encircling the clouds of Artabassa, reflected her female eyes like human stars, like constellations of her enigmatic eyes, this knowledge of life and death locked away perhaps by her retina which could see beyond skin and flesh. But she had not surrendered her secret to him. He still did not know how to live, how to die. And inside her, he was floating, uncertain. To kill her or to kill himself? The one he killed was not the one he should have killed to be free. She would outlive all the ones he would meet. She was the bright star of this other world where, imprisoned by Esther's eyes, in spite of his blaspheming, desecrating those eyes, he could not help adoring their unattainable flicker and sinking deep into a misty delirium which had the face and appearance of a woman. He felt like a dwarf kneeling at the feet of the goddess of the sky eyeing him scornfully with infinite radiance.

"I work to forget."

Esther had not spared a single one of his cells; he was devoured by mental illness; he could not understand anymore; he saw everything through her; he could not live outside of her, of her hold; it was as though she was not dead, as though he was not separated from her forever, as though there had been something immortal in her which he had not been able to destroy and which could not be cured in him.

"A witch. . . ."

His eyes were bulging. It was as if he could penetrate the night. She had withstood love, hate, separation, mourning, adventures, forgetting, alcohol, asceticism, mysticism, crime, refusal, all this self-denial this man had tried so he could dissociate himself from his obsession, and today, she went on sparkling inside him. Did she still have a body or just an aura which, even deprived of a body by death, was stubbornly bringing the man back to these golden spots, to this bedazzlement? He could not remember the curve of her back or her breasts; he no longer dared to brush up, even lightly, against any woman, undress any woman, because not one would have her blondness, her mucous membranes; he would always be comparing; in his opinion she surpassed all women; he was afraid to disappear forever, to sink into this dead woman. There is nothing more beautiful for a man than your body during love. Love with you is fantastic, he would marvel. Your body makes a man happy beyond measure. Your body is beautiful. So alive.

At which moment did she stop living?

Esther wanders through an unbearable radiance. On the eve of her death, she had announced, "You're going to betray me." Her eyes were glaring red above the flame of the candle that Charles had placed between Esther and himself to light their farewell dinner. From then on, he would never again be able to tell her that he loved her; he would only be able to say it to another, thinking about her, mistaking another for her in the course of moments of desperation, such as this one in this park when everything is becoming confused in his brain as if he were drunk. He looks at the stranger.

"Your name is . . . ?"

"Olga."

How far will a man be driven by a woman? Does she make him descend into his subconscious? is she his reflection? When he faces her, what terror freezes him, forces him to retreat, to climb back up to the body's surface and, disillusioned, to search somewhere else for that moment of recognition when, too close to the lights emitted by the fusion's rays, he saw his own madness reflected in this other self, in this blazing woman? Is it possible to return from there even once, just once? Do we ever return from the realm of mothers whose crestfallen son we will always be? the creature with the shattered nerves? the witness to our mortal destiny and a night swept up by currents, by swirls of mad stars? Madness cruises relentlessly, makes us thirsty, makes us hungry, puts sparkles in our eyes during some tense face-to-face, in the midst of a limitless void. He would be left with scars like those of a burn victim. He should never have let her come so deep inside him. He had tried to throw her out, but she was the eternity and the hell where the Christian faith of Charles de Roquemont's ancestors had made sinners believe they would roast forever. And Charles was still burning in the consuming fire, in the agony where no presence is ever as near as the absence which no longer releases us from this union between a human being and a ghost. Was it the face of madness? Had he seen it? Does it have a face? Was he mad? Olga turns away from the smell of alcohol and fire on his breath. What is left to live, once we have roamed the world? What is left that is still as limitless as the absolute for those who have not yet attained forgiveness? Those whose beloveds have left them with nothing but the white-hot fragments of the inferno that wrecked their sanity when the shelter that the other could have been, were love possible, was snatched away from them and the lovers were propelled into a nightmare from which not even their excruciating pains could wake them again?

He had gone there once, maybe only once, but he could not return from there. He had been the road in the storm; he had been a November-night moon resembling a purple sun wrapped in storm clouds; he had been the forests, the rocks shimmering in the cool water of a river just before winter turns it to ice; he had been the house where Esther would never reside, the countries where she would never live; he had played the game of metamorphosis; inside him, she had visited empty rooms, isolated villages; she had wanted to rest there, to sleep in a bed, to eat in a kitchen, to listen to music in a living room, but to what other house, to what other country, to what other village bring the visitor, except to the madness which clung to the man like a shadow? Nowhere had the woman felt secure; everywhere outlines, shapes were shifting, surfaces were no longer defined, speech fluctuated, each facial expression contradicted what the mouth was enunciating.

Sometimes, over there, the man knelt, became smaller, blended in with the dragonflies he would observe on summer nights in the marsh, in a microscopic world whose dimensions were reduced to those of a blade of grass. Over there, Charles would tell Esther, eyes closed, while kissing her: "I see dragonflies everywhere; there are thousands, millions of them . . . I don't see you anymore; I don't feel you anymore . . . I'm not with you anymore, I'm with millions of dragonflies." Thus, sometimes, over there, the only place where he could find shelter was in a blade of grass on which he would concentrate during his efforts at miniaturization induced by the attacks during which, otherwise, he would not have known anymore how to defuse the hate growing within him, brutally rising toward his hands, toward his eyes. Then, seeing him again, out of the blue go from the size of a dragonfly to the size of a mad giant, Esther would shiver. . . .

"You send shivers down my spine. . . ."

Olga, staring at the man seated across from her in the park, is calculating her chances of seeing him again. For her, this Parisian does not have a name yet. She is probing his eyes; she is trying to decipher his forehead. The stranger is telling her about art, about creation, but what Olga hears comes from another place which she is ready to visit without needing to name it, because, if we were to define our inner confusion, we would never be able to give in to it, we would be aghast, we would not, of our own free will, step across some zones which will make us come face-to-face with the irrational, the passion which uses our appetite for life to justify the lure of death.

Perhaps Olga, doomed from the start, will excite him to conquest, a man drawn to women he thinks are all the same; perhaps she will make him believe that he will know how to reach a woman's being, to wrap himself with it as with a pelt? What do we know of our desire? She will climax, her body, her genitals will no longer be those of a woman but those of this man who will hit her, will prick her, maybe will kill her, and the delight will make her so dizzy that Olga will not think of reacting. Is Olga ready? She goes ahead, defenseless, speechless, meets him, just as he wants her, outside of the social world, outside of herself, outside of the law, as though already she were giving up life and as though she were letting herself fall under the drug of an imaginary salvation. He takes her out of reality. She was prepared. She can love in madness and in death.

What is sadism? What is impotence? It is this man to whom a woman calls out and who will never answer because he cannot be a man. It is when there is no more distinction between human beings, but only a dull hatred which levels everything, crushes everything; it is the sterile world of those who hate their own skin, their own heart, and will never reproduce again; it is the man who, after having bashed against a bench the skull of the woman he was not giving himself the right to love, puts out his own eyes like Oedipus. . . .

Esther was buried on a roadside, at the foot of a pink-bricked Protestant church, in a cemetery exposed to the gusty winds from the desolate mountains of the northeast United States, three hours from the Canadian border. In this region, the nights are often bright, spangled with stars more remote than anywhere else, as if over there the sky were farther up. Charles had never gone back to the grave site. He knew that the marker stood out against the edge of a forest and that, not far off, in a field, horses neighed all night long as though they were talking to the dead woman, as though they were celebrating her beauty stilled forever by the act of a madman. Sometimes he would dream that he was going back to Vermont. He would be walking aimlessly on the road to the village, toward the horizon; he could not feel the icy wind stinging his hands, his cheeks, his feet. After a few miles of roaming, he would stop; he would lay down on the frozen ground and sob. He remembered the old farm with the blue wood and white brick front. He remembered the moonlight and the serenity of the stars.

The dog, a golden Labrador, would accompany him and that woman when she was still alive and was showing America's vast landscape to the European. She would show the Frenchman tombstones in a cemetery that dated back to the time of the American Revolution. Charles would look at the names and the dates engraved during the eighteenth century; he would shiver. He would raise his head to the starry sky. Could it be that which was already connecting him to Esther was not on this earth, but this sky through which he flew in a Boeing, over the Atlantic, to meet her and that now, since her death, he was constantly staring at because from up there, it is believed, the dead signal to us? Does this Olga seated in a park in Paris look like Esther? The man examines the details, the width of the nostrils, the lobe of the ear, a fragile nature. He cannot help comparing the French woman to the American woman whom he had loved as passionately as he had hated.

Esther was born in Hanover, on the other side of the Connecticut River which separates Vermont from New Hampshire. She was one of those New England aristocrats whose Puritan sobriety and bearing have been immortalized in nineteenth- and early twentieth-century paintings found in Boston museums. He had been madly in love with the death that he had carefully engineered for Esther all these months during which he had patiently managed to turn her against life, before deciding one night, in Artabassa, in western Canada, to finish her off. . . .

He had lighted two candles which had burned until morning and the white melted wax had left nothing more than a residue above which the candle flame swayed like the breath of the dying woman breathing her last on the bed in this steel and glass hotel where, on the twentieth floor, the man and the woman had kissed for the last time with a tenderness that would make the crime even more barbaric. "It's sweet . . .," he would whisper in tears while he was gagging her with a napkin. "It's sweet . . .," he would repeat. What does sadism mean? Just what is a madman's impotence overwhelmed by love? Just what does it mean when a man turns into a wolf? Since his return to France, he did not know how to get rid of Esther, the woman he had murdered. He had stomach, liver, and intestinal problems; she filled his insides. He couldn't breathe anymore, couldn't sleep anymore, couldn't swallow anything anymore; he had indigestion, bouts of diarrhea and vomiting. He suffered from depression; he couldn't remove this weight that was smothering him. His eyes blinked continuously under the gaze of this woman who, night and day, was accusing him, was making him defend himself, making him prove to her repeatedly that he still felt more love for her, yes, still more, that he would never exhaust this mad love. She was insatiable. He did not know how to placate her, how to convince her that he loved her. She did not seem to realize that his nerves were fragile. He would become furious at the least contradiction. He was unbalanced. His mind was "deranged," as the boys at his school used to say about him long ago. She had defied him; she demanded that he act as if he were normal; it was as if she refused to realize that he was too "simple," a "half-wit," an alcoholic, as well as an artist, someone who had difficulty organizing words for thinking and who often only caught their sounds, their din, these booming voices from invisible sources that wanted to harm him, that frightened him and ordered him that night, in the Artabassa hotel room, to finally silence them.

For a long time afterwards, he could still see with remorse the blue wood porch from which, looking over the valley at sundown, the couple would admire the force of the silver-grey river's current. Charles felt that the driving energy of the hundreds of lakes and rivers from the mountains simmered in his blood, lifted him, brought him back in time, made him a brother to wild presences, as if he had known the Pawtucket tribe which, before the arrival of the first Europeans, inhabited southern New Hampshire and as if the frost-covered trees reminded Charles of the shapes, the souls of the primitive inhabitants of the Sokikois' territory, these Indians that Americans today call "Native Americans." Over there, so close to the great forests, Charles did not feel like going back to France, did not feel like crossing the ocean again. He was hibernating in the confusion of his imaginary geography where, giving free rein to his dreams of adventures, he would mix all together the caimans, the snakes, the leopards, the reindeer, the beavers, the ringdoves, the parrots, the pine trees, the palm trees, the oaks, the wild cherry trees, the maples, the sassafras in an archaic winter which he could taste with his tongue, with his sense of smell, with his fingers on this woman, Esther the dearly loved, mother-territory where, snuggled up in her, sheltered from the climate, he fiercely projected his visions of a little boy with arrested mental development.

After the murder, he had wanted to catch up with the adolescence, the youth that he had thought he could skip. He had lived in the bars, the discotheques, the hotel rooms of Paris, Berlin, Montreux, Geneva, Milan, but this dead woman was as much a part of him as God is part of a believer, while hell was relentlessly scratching at Charles's belly, plowing his nape, his temples, with the speed of a racing car whose wheels, during his dissipations, were running over his muscles, over the bones of the man crushed by the impossibility of atonement and by his stubborn insistence on reaching the conscience he lacked and which he had tried to take away from the one who had been for him its physical radiance, its mirror image, as though he had wanted to emigrate into her, trade beings with her, become her, have her soul as though he had thought he could reclaim in this feminine reflection of himself the traces of the reality to which those who have lost their mind can no longer have access; and as though he never was able to get near enough the mirror reflecting fleeting glimmers and as though he had only been capable of breaking, pulverizing what is real, oh! those cold eyes, harshness of this woman whose child he had wanted to be and who, closing herself off from him, resisted him, severe, haughty.

There will come a day when the regressive man will drift toward the icy parts of his heart, his personal polar extremity that he longs to feel melting away as if, on a chance meeting, a woman could revive in him the mother from whom this son had not been weaned, whose enormous breasts he had not suckled enough, savored enough, eaten enough. Oh! prison! prison! He had gnawed with jealous, carnivorous teeth each of its fleshy bars, each millimeter of the neckline into the freckles of this skin and, thinking he could escape, he had sliced through its pulsing veins under the delicate throat which had gushed with bubbling blood. He was still seeing crimson; to protect himself from the sight, he shaded his eyes. Olga asked him:

"Do your eyes hurt?"

He shivers nervously. Olga wants to get up, go toward him, take him by the shoulder, make the flow of life she wanted to give back to him stream within him. She senses that Charles is miserable. Rich with the vitality that she has been saving up for too long, she assesses, without scorn, the other's need.

Soon it will all come hemorrhaging back, will once again become the crimson, vampiric realm of a cutthroat. . . .

He remembered rows of markers on the heights of Norwich from which the couple, at dusk, liked to watch the landscape taking on a reddish hue, the flickering lights of the long university buildings, the foot of the hill sloping toward the inn and the road. Esther, alive or dead, could magnetize equally the air, the wind, the clouds, the forest, the fields which, to the northeast, over there, past the Atlantic Ocean, surround the towns and the villages, and mark the broadening of the earth, the broadening of the view, the sensation that a European has of not being in Europe anymore but in America and, for the exiled man, Esther had been an allegory of America, where he had traveled through a woman like an explorer over virgin territory. For months, he could not tell the difference between her and the snow or hail gusts that swirled and lashed against their faces when he and Esther would go out, would go from the porch to the garage, an old barn, a mass of humidity and darkness. Once settled in the little Japanese car, the couple would ride toward the heights of Brag Hill or toward Woodstock. Charles could no longer tell the difference between Esther and the Ompompanoosuc which, night and day, would swell at the end of the garden, behind the birches, with a rumbling sound that the European could not stand anymore. It was blood circulating through arteries, veins, blood vessels. Charles would hear the sound of the river rushing toward the lakes and the dams. Some nights, the exhausted man wanted to halt, in this moist, gluey, liquid woman, this biological river which he then dreamed of silencing and subduing. Esther's blood would have gone on coagulating, until that moment when the killer's hate for the other's life becomes absolute . . . when Esther, not understanding why, seeing his mad eyes penetrating the invisible and directed at her belly, would flinch. She would say in amazement:

"I don't feel good. I don't know what's the matter with me."

He would not answer. Coming from the river, the whistling reached his ears, grew in his head, became rushing waves of blood.

Simultaneously memories parade within the miserable man captivated by the beautiful face of a stranger whose resemblance to the dearly loved Esther is poignant. Standing in front of Olga, he is facing an insurmountable obstacle. She is a closed woman through whom he wants at all costs to find an opening, an entrance.

She had begun to froth with blood-flecked foam, to bleed as if she had been the representation of the overflow that the sick man had been unable to contain within him any longer.

Under the influence of the man who had taken her away from Brendan, her husband, Esther had changed; she had abandoned her friends, her family, anyone in a position to help her; she had no more points of reference in this madness of a man who was casting her out of herself and, like a bum who sleeps in parks and eats out of garbage cans, she had little by little given herself over to a life-style of self-destruction; she had given in as her personality was gradually deteriorating, drained by that of the sick man to whom she sometimes felt she was giving shelter, not in her and Brendan's house, but in this woman's fragile state of the being, in the private inner space where the mental problems of the desperate man she would have liked to save were torturing her. It was as though she had hospitalized him inside herself, inside her body, which was attempting to define itself, to become a refuge for this derelict. She wanted to rescue Charles from his roving, from his expulsion from the society where he would have committed infractions, would have eventually stolen, cheated, committed crimes, under the influence of the urges that impelled him to fulfill his sense of emptiness, the need which drove him toward this woman. He was attempting to be cured of this illness, maybe of this hatred, and he was trying to love, but he behaved in love as though he did not know how to read or write; he was weakened; he would drag himself, exhausted, illiterate, into the other. He would surrender, given over to all sorts of ineptitudes and, abandoning the idea of begging this force, he would have left, would have returned to Paris, would have slept outside, near subway openings or in entranceways of apartment buildings; there was no more law in him, no more structure, nothing left; he could only cling to this woman, identify with her, with the tenseness he could feel in her, as in an adventure where he had the impression of continuously hesitating between sex and death, of doubting, of never knowing how to choose reality. He felt like strangling her . . . he did not know how to communicate . . . how to find his way toward the other, how to speak to her, how to listen to her, how to caress her, how to kiss her. Of Esther he knew only the effects of possession. Amid a lack of tenderness, amid a lack of truth, where naming one another is impossible, they steadfastly held on to each other in a passion where their roles faded into silence, went from impotence to the impossible where the man would look at himself in this woman, in this mirror of his fear, of his inhibition, of his feminization, as though Esther were castrating him, as though, silently, she were avenging herself for being inhaled, sucked by the eagerness of the vampire who was taking her in. The river flowed below the kitchen windows. Esther and Charles would be rigidly seated at the table, facing each other, in their motionless duel. . . .

"Olga . . . your name is Olga?"

"And you?"

"How important is my name? I don't even have one anymore. . . ."

"Yes, you do. Tell me."

"At random . . . any . . . Charles . . . François . . . Louis. . . ."

"Names of kings. . . ."

Just what is the wind that rings in your ears like sleigh bells? What is this shrillness? How can memory be plugged so that no sound comes out of it, so that nothing of this woman can survive? To kill her, oh! To continue to kill, to kill so as to endure no longer the scream that she howled like a woman undergoing the pain of childbirth when she let go of him, when she aborted, when he fell from her as if he were a thing, a package, this pathetic object rendered inanimate, the dead fetus that she was expelling, that she refused to keep inside her. She had betrayed him. She loved another. She had seen Brendan again. . . . It was going to snow. All day long, Esther would devour brownies, muffins, strawberry ice cream, sugar to sweeten bitterness. The twists and turns of the Ompompanoosuc and the road enclosed the rolling tree-covered hills that separate mountainous Vermont from flatter New Hampshire. Esther could feel herself the target of Charles's rage, who, for hours, in the kitchen or in the bedroom, would observe her as though he were silently accusing her of not being a source of life. What else was he proposing during these endless days except the possibility of death for him or for her? Esther was at bay. She was begging for warmth, a hand, security; she would come near Charles, would brush a timid finger against the man's skin, hair; she had hoped for all the love in the world from him. But he would control her with his vengeful, indifferent eyes. Esther, frightened, would back away. He would be lying in wait. Soon he would be pouncing; all they had left to do was to hypnotize each other, to come together while they waited, amid the fantasies that precede a gradually more and more threatening act. How those days seemed monotonous, all brown from the hills and the forests, all grey from the movement of the river that ran toward the horizon.

In the heat of the Parisian summer, Olga, so far away from America, is slipping into the at times glib, at times almost mute tête-à-tête during which, in the eyes of the man, alternated indescribable scenery, a forgotten country, fury, light, darkness, by turns brightening and darkening Charles's expression. Why does he continue to stare at her with such persistence, as though he were constantly about to ask something which at the last minute he would refrain from formulating, held in check by some apprehension? This woman is not yet ready or is not the one he is addressing. The man needs more patience to leave the other, to give her up, to return to this country, to become familiar with his own language; to resign himself to ask of this Olga, to ask again for what Esther had been for him but which not one, no, not one, never, could ever give him again, this mixture of sensual explosion that had overwhelmed him when Esther, wife of Brendan, whom she adored, had been willing to undress in the room tinged in silver by the river's reflection, and to lie down, naked, beside Charles, who had held his breath.

Swept along by the waves of the Ompomopanoosuc, Olga is hypnotized by the red visions of the man haunted by blood; she gives in to the appeal of this madness which has been slumbering within her and which dreams of waking up, of bursting out, of relieving the inflammations, the reddening sores that Olga feels herself secreting with the contractions of her belly where something is guiding her, something that all women vaguely feel they have in common with fire, water, air, earth, volcanoes, savagery, hurricanes, which prevent her from backing off when their mad swirls approach her eyes, her ears, envelop her, and, oppressed, amid the pounding, she guesses that the time for passion has arrived. . . .

Esther lifted her eyes toward the light dappled with mist, striped with black or light green bushes, fringed with mountainous peaks smoothed out by winter where, until sudden nightfall, the bare scenery was filled with shifting hues, tossed about by gusts of wind. Accompanied by her dog, Esther would walk along the sunlit road, meandering along the river where, with her eyes, the tired woman would try to regain contact with life, fleeing everywhere, taken away toward the east, toward the west by the setting sun's arrows piercing the forests and the fields with gold. Against the mountainous landscape Esther could see the outline of a shape which she did not know how to approach anymore, a shape which sometimes took on a human appearance. Esther had begun loving Charles as the incarnation of the height of the sky and the clouds forever distant in the iridescence of these mountains and these hills that invite communion with grandiose nature created in God's image . . . as the erection of the swelling earth whose mystical accents, not fully forgotten, would vaguely reemerge in Esther's daydreams. There was something elementary in this probably sick European that the American had just met that urged this dreamy woman to try to achieve, as a result of her fusion with him, a rapture where we disintegrate into atoms, where we become reunited with mother-matter, where our individuality is no longer perceptible, where there is obedience to one's tendency for renunciation. We are not born yet, not even conceived yet. That was how she was dreaming of being united to him, in the infinite loss of being, in the infinite deliverance; dreaming how this sick man would grant this depressed woman the gift which, when she was near him, Esther knew she was ready to receive. She did not want to be spared any longer. She was burning alive. The torture was dragging on. Body and soul were rushing toward that moment when we are reacquainted with our origins from which the flesh, whatever the age, never manages to learn to get free. Temptation draws us toward a void that excites our desire for death. If we kill, it is because our victim has mysteriously asked us to do it. He is sure of it. . . . She had asked for it right away, as soon as she had looked into these two eyes that were going to reply to her as if they were merging with hers. For him, Esther the American had been so much taller than any woman ever is. She had been the nourishing earth, the depths of rivers and lakes, the humus of the underbrush, the other side of the bridge where she would shine, her clothes damp with the rain from their walk. Her skin was soft as the down of a hazel-nut tree leaf. He would brush his lips against her fresh cheek. He believed that Esther was still these paths where they had walked together in the fresh air along the river's edge, in these damp chilly bowels of the earth that he would never forget and from which, in his memory, he could still absorb this woman's dew; his heart was still flooded by a surge of instincts; drop by drop, he would sip the gilt of the day. Thus for a long time, Charles would bathe in the strength he still drew from her by scrutinizing Europe's earth and sky for hours. Charles would always need to come back to the United States to breathe, to magnify its forests, its mountains for as long as he would live, but why is it that we understand later, when it is too late, the reasons for these remissions that hurt more than our incurable hurt? Why is it that intermittently we rediscover conscience, music, realize that we participated with all our cruelty in death, in the pain of the world without end where, no sooner dispelled, despair pounces on us again, even more violently, once more crushes us more harshly, reignites in us the flame of murder? He was remembering the black sky, the blue clouds of the shady state in which jealousy had poisoned him, over there, hour by hour. Hour by hour, he had repeated to himself the sentences that Esther and Brendan, back together, must have whispered to each other in the house they had built up on Brag Hill with a view of the subtle shadings of the dark, flaming sky.

"I love you more every day."

"I love you too, Brendan."

Something that Charles would have never said to any woman because it would have been a lie; he hated all women too much and Esther, the too-dearly loved, even more; for him, not one of them would be as radiantly beautiful as the American girl had been in this misery where Charles, kneeling before her in the evening, would rest his head on the thighs of too blonde, too satiny Esther, and, near her, he knew nothing other than becoming a child again incapable of telling this goddess that he felt too small, too small before her to love her as a man loves a woman. . . .

But in one night he made up for it all and 874 times he had made love to her, and she could not insult him anymore, call him an impotent anymore, compare him to Brendan, that ram. . . . And he had smeared himself in her all night long and he had made her scream, moan; he had spread himself out over Esther's genitals; he had dipped himself in her as in milk, and he had been a blood-wolf, a werewolf lapping up the blood of this disemboweled woman with her throat cut, as if he were running across a wheat field; and she had opened herself up to the tumescent penis, pointed like a lance, and she had spurted, blonde, in the bloody rite, in the Artabassa hotel room, all night long, up there, farther north, farther west, in the midst of the desolate spaces of this sparsely populated Canada where he had taken her, on this honeymoon of horror, where he had taken her away from Brendan forever, where he had sullied her 874 times; he had loved her 874 times the way a wolf kills a goat; where he had covered himself with her blood like a dog that has tasted blood; amid the bloodshed where he had satisfied her 874 times he had sated himself with this woman, had done it again 874 times, had ejaculated in the blood and the screams of this woman whose belly was bleeding, yes, had reveled in the horror of feeding on warm blood, had drunk bowls and bowls of her blood, had wiped up the blood with her panties and brassiere, had planted himself in her like a stake, had wanted to crucify her, to torture her, had turned his penis into the cutting edge of an ax splitting her, and she was dripping from her arms and legs full of holes, and the madman was a pocket knife which opened the jugular vein at the neck, and the murderer drew a glassful of warm blood which he drank with the rage with which his penis was stiffening inside the one who was asking for mercy, who was yelling "no, no . . ." that it was too much . . . begging him to stop, but he had become a man, finally a man with the fire of a lover, a raving madman, a bloodthirsty madman being spattered with living blood, and he was climaxing, finally, he was climaxing like a man with spasms under which he could feel her slowly dying and he took pains to last, last the whole of this night in the Artabassa hotel, inside her, inside her distended vagina which it was no longer necessary to hurt, which no longer felt anything in Charles's mouth. He was collecting the blood of the violated woman who was losing her strength and who, even wounded, would come nearer to him, would go ever nearer, nearer to the monster that, to the end, she thought she could appease, but he was enjoying himself too much; he could no longer spit her back out, calm himself; the drops of black blood stained the carpet; he was moaning with pleasure in her softness; her skin was so soft and his penis was a javelin, a spearhead ever sharper, but she would scream louder and louder; she would call out for help and the blood would fill her mouth, muffle the sounds, obstruct her throat; she was suffocating; he was crying; he wiped his penis, his hands on the sheet; he had a morbid desire to linger, to continue rummaging through these viscera, to eat the raw flesh, to hide in these feminine organs, to prowl furtively around in them, in the dawn which was beginning to shine on the bloody scene where the demented man was in a mucus bedroom, in the muscular, fatty, aqueous room of a red, broken-into castle, where, with his massive jaws of an anthropoid, he was trying to reach the cervix, trying to come out of this woman using his prominent front teeth, the way one uses dangerous weapons capable of inflicting mortal wounds. Inside her he had regained energy; he had renewed himself; he was primitive, a simian predator, a brute with Mongoloid characteristics, with molars twice as large as those of a gorilla. When, at the hotel, he saw himself in the bathroom mirror, he did not recognize himself; he thought about his mother; he burst into tears.

The lapping sounds of the Ompompanoosuc sparkled in a golden bend, under the lights in the sky.

Just what is madness? An impulse taking the place of the sun's rays and glowing so bright in our brain that it is as though this light were clubbing us, as though the glare from its infinite reflections would not dim anymore, as though the shock were repeated indefinitely, leaving us numb. Charles was obsessed with the shimmering play of light on the brambles, the birch trees, the ash trees, the fir trees, the hay fields, the White Mountains, the Green Mountains of the forgotten Vermont village where Esther's body was splitting into the pieces of this solar puzzle. To the ends of the landscape, she appeared disfigured, dismembered by her own demagnification, splintered in Charles's mind who could no longer escape his passion for this woman whom he could love only as an imaginary being, only as an ideal, only in his obsession with severing her, with belittling her in order to be able to dominate her, to make her be quiet, to become her master, to no longer feel less than nothing, a chimpanzee before this queen whom he adored to the point of premeditating killing her so as finally to be relieved of this superhuman burden of adoration.

The haze, the mist shrouded reality. Charles was dreaming of soaring toward a superior world where feelings are free of the weight of the body; where he could kiss silky hair without pulling it, without yanking it out of anger; where he could kiss the beautiful mouth without ripping it to pieces; where there would be a relief from the madness which will overtake us again, later, when once more life will assail us with the urges that would engulf us in a woman if we did not fight back, if we did not know how to pounce on her, yes, if we do not know how to distinguish the good one from the bad one, the true one from the false one, if the one we love does not come forth in time, the unreal one who will exist only as the forbidden one, the untouchable one, different from all the ones who stick to our fingernails, to our skin, to our tongue, to our saliva, in a loathsome mixture where we never see her, where maybe we catch a glimpse of her in the blinding flash of an orgasm, but it is always the others; she is not the one we nab, she is never the one, the one we thought that we loved so closely, that we held in our arms, that we licked all over the face and body of another, whose soulless substance is left in our hands like a pitiful, empty, useless object, to be thrown away because the one we want is a perception of what has no flesh, no breath, is like God, in this long martyrdom we have been enduring eternally; as though we refused to be an orphan; as though we could not be a man for any of these women; as though we were only a son mad with hate from having been abandoned by the childhood which, before our eyes, continues to encircle with a halo the clouds, the sky, savagely, yes, savagely! in the space where only airplanes and birds fly and where no angel will rush toward us to forgive us. . . .

He was perturbed about Esther; she had 874 bodies that had to be eliminated before discovering her substance, before seizing her heart, before taking it away to hell where he can suck her with an unpunished voracity, where he can feel like a woman, a woman and a man, all-powerful, relieved of this void, this need, relieved of this desire, relieved of her, but he would have let himself relent if she had held him tight against her to make him enter her female belly, to house him, snuggled up inside her, in this womb which must have been huge like the red castle where he had imagined burrowing his hands deep enough to feel the sticky entrails palpitate in his disemboweler's hands. . . .

⸢6⸣

Why won't Olga back off? Is she moving toward him? A woman, some summer evening, out of boredom, chooses a maniac, a sadist as mentor. The Paris street is dirty. The magnetism of the great loners suddenly captures you. Trembling with impatience, you risk seeking from a crazed stranger the electrical shocks, the violent vibrations of an impending threat of death. Your whole body, your sex, complies.

Some summer evening, a predator stops you. You were walking in Monceau Park. You were daydreaming, the air was heavy, it must have felt good to be at the beach. But your film script kept you in Paris, in your apartment, near your dictionaries, your lexicons, your grammars, an atlas, your cats, your furniture, your place mats. You think that you are never surrounded with enough books, with enough erudition, with enough encyclopedias to reassure you, to dare create on your own because you are always afraid of making a mistake, of not finding just the right word, but here, you can feel it, you are going to leave the language that is written, read, spoken, and return to the other language, the one before words, sentences. Something all wet, all warm. A growl, a clucking. You will be consumed, body and soul, by sensation. He is coming nearer. How to translate this other language into yours? At this stage, what is it? You are illuminated by his gaze. He appraises you from the blue lightning of his eyes. He exudes animality, his and yours. You rush up, willing, drunk. His hands are too large, his fleshy mouth seems to overshadow his mind. His square shoulders contrast with the limberness of his hips toward which his slender torso tapers.

The stream no longer rushes to the river; the twists and turns of the Ompompanoosuc River no longer flow into the straight width of the Connecticut River bordered with frost-covered pine and elm trees. The houses are no longer covered with white or grey shingles like the Victorian houses of New England. Here, there is no scenery for him, only the obsessive need of entering orifices, of diminishing the woman still ignorant of the fact that, for him, she is only these holes, this gaping hole, this vagina, this anus, their hope to be filled, to be jolted, profaned, forced by the bestiality of a man mad about a body which will fall to pieces, will never fit back together, will never again be a person, will never again have anything human in these pieces of her, these breasts, this navel, this tongue, this saliva that he will seize with his teeth and his jaws, determined to cut, grate, lacerate, mutilate. . . .

He can only love transsexually; for him to love is to violate the physiology that designates gender, the masculine, the feminine, in the flesh, in the limits of the mortal body; he can only bite, scratch, scrape, tear beyond wrathful, vengeful love where he tries to take hold of the other, to annihilate the other, to drown in the other with the gluttony of a madman.

Five years ago, Esther told Charles about her friends from Stafford, from Woodstock, from Hanover, from Lyme, from the neighboring towns, but she also spoke to him of Brendan, her physicist husband who had worked at Los Alamos in New Mexico and who belonged to the Society of Atomic Scientists. In the United States, each day this group of scientists calculates the time variations which separate us from the threat of an apocalyptic nuclear war. She also spoke about a New York friend, Berny; he had just had an automobile accident because he was depressed by the idea of having to leave New York, his hometown, to move to the Midwest, Ohio—a region of reactionary farmers, Esther would exclaim. Charles listened, moody. "Not everyone is rich in Vermont," Esther said. "Many poor people live in cabins or trailers, almost as in the nineteenth century." She also said, "I don't feel secure here. Violence is all around; people are too isolated. At any moment, the sound of firing, a rifle shot can break the silence; there are suicides, murders, incest, sons who batter their mothers. . . ." Darkness was approaching. Charles's face lost its playful look. His eyes were no longer visible. He pulled back. Esther, seated in front of him, had the feeling he was spying on her.

From which lining of radiance does memory derive? A shadowy triangle blots out Olga's face. On the Norwich tombs covered with snow a few names appear at the top of the stones: Tabatha, Howard, Katherine, or a date: 1895. Beyond the dam and the covered bridge, at the end of the cemetery, there is a view of the Green Mountains through sparkles in the ash trees radiant with frost from which there rained drops of sunshine whenever the wind blew.

In late afternoon, around Lake Fairlee, the distant mountains would turn pink before turning brown, blue. The river glinted red as it moved along a curve through the islands of fir trees heavy with snow from the last storm. Esther was driving toward Lyme. On each side of the road, the reflected sunset blanketed the ice with shades of rust, orange, and red. Charles no longer knows how to dispel these twilight colors which, superimposed, appear and disappear on Olga's face against the sunlight. Over there, where he had spent so many months loving, hating, it was not the hectic life of Boston, New York, Los Angeles, San Francisco, or Chicago; it was the very treacherous calm of these blue and faded pink horizons, these lands of mirages. . . .

7

Suddenly Olga wants to live, live at all costs. She is anxious. She has
forgotten how to live. She wanted to restrain her body, her sexuality,
her instinct. But is it possible to restrain the subconscious? Charles is
leading the way and she is ready. It will be sweet to be part of him, to
obliterate reality, to sink into cushions, into pillows where, eyes half
shut, in the pink glimmer of a night-light, while it is snowing outside,
you let go, you are not tense anymore, stress vanishes. And then the
other's voice cozily reverberates in you, you breathe, you give yourself over to the tone of his whisper. You are beautiful, he tells you; it is
the moment for orgasm; you are alive; desire seeps into you; you feel
something quivering, lengthen, harden; you are not alone anymore;
little by little his penis brings you peace. The man's voice snuggles
against your heart and makes it beat again. He is the one you were
waiting for, his seduction, just as you pictured him, just as you
imagined it. You do not see the blackness of the lonely night unlighted
by house, village, town. Nevertheless, in the middle of summer, this
winter night is going to pierce your liver, your ears, your head. In spite
of your dream, you hear its engine noise as if you were driving frantically toward this elopement at the center of progressive extinction,
progressive regression. You think you are deeper inside yourself; in
fact, you are outside, in exile. You are driving aimlessly; you have left
yourself and you are following the occasional light signals which,
passing through the gaze of this stranger, penetrate your night. You
are certain of the disturbances in the nervous system of the one who
flashes these beams in your direction as in the olden days wreckers
would light flares on the rocks of the shores where the ships they were
going to pillage had run aground. The countries that he will lead you
through are uninhabited expanses, devastated zones, a limitless
absence. . . . For hours you will persist obstinately without discovering, on the stern face, any sign of life, any reaction. Your vision will go
blurry; reality will seem more and more fuzzy, problematic. Inside and
outside will be separated by something like a windowpane covered
with steam. You will have crossed the border; you will have entered
his territory. All will be dark. You will begin to look like him; you will
not be able to speak except in his language, and you will not communicate other than in this mad language; you will no longer know
where delirium begins and ends. Long winter. Your flickering intellect
will no longer give off enough light. You will open your eyes wide to

explore the realm of the night of the spirit where, as though the body were dead, we walk, eat, kiss, tell our dreams from the previous night out loud, automatically, and your eyes fixed in amazement on this empty man. And, in order to survive, you will continue to invent him; you will refuse to come out of the madness that will have you in its grip.

When we have nowhere to go, feeling distraught, ineffectual, not knowing who we should admit our failure to, desiring nothing, feeling guilty about avoiding life, there will always be this cold north country of the earth where it is darker than anywhere else, where the light shines less often, for shorter periods, where people drink themselves into oblivion to warm their icy innards, where language, up there, is limited to the few words they can barely write, up there, barely read because in these defeated regions there is no will to think; sons and daughters of these fallow spaces where sometimes, forsaken, bereft of help, it is possible to die from cold and hunger, imprisoned by this endless isolation where the only people who congregate are outcasts, failures, misfits who have nothing to say to one another and who, in their spectral bodies, stumble around under the burden of an infinite impotence as if they were crawling toward an impossible goal. So there, at the heart of these regressive territories, in the night of consciousness, we have the sensation of being able to meet up again with our fellow creature, to know in his company the fusion which is like a balm to our pain in this state of confusion where the blow is softened, where we no longer know, where we no longer need to know, where we no longer need to struggle, to persevere, where we can go blind; the only thing that matters is for anxiety and doubt to abate, for wild imagination to stir us, for impulse to show the way; we grab hold of a hand, to one of these people residing in the lands of the lower world, to these drives, to these emotional whirls, to these stirrings which we have lost the courage to resist.

8

Olga weakens. She is not taking into account the shabbiness of the slightly deceitful but passionately attentive, observant stranger. She yields. Give me life, give me life, she implores, like a redemption, while the shadow intensifies, encircles the vulnerability of this woman who is beginning to explore the world's north countries where crows fly above the blinking lights of the land of declining reason, swept away by a perpetual wind, where bones are frozen by the melting snow swirling in an endless winter, soaking the ground where we skid on icy patches, where we stagger, cautiously walking toward faint lights which make us believe that, in the distance, there is a house that twinkles, that we will be able to enter, where we will be warm, and where we will stay. . . . But the more we expect to find a haven in this bad weather, and the more we imagine we are near our goal, the farther away we are. We are denied satisfaction. The more we invoke the place, the less likely it is to materialize, the less likely there will be life in this death. We vainly beg the black flash of his eyes for friendliness while the mad animal lies in wait for us, invites us to run after him, while he arouses pain within us, while he causes us distress, always more hostile, more sadistic, more smiling, in this hold his cruelty has over our fear of never being able to be free of savagery, to rest, to save ourselves. Her heart racing, Olga answers:

"There are chance encounters that can make you lose your mind."

He answers as though he wanted to warn her, "Dangerous encounters. . . ."

The enemy is here, invisible. Waves of ice. It is cold down in your belly. You feel as though each pore of your skin, of your face, is being studied by the maniac; you feel as though his eyes are carving you up. . . .

For Esther the American, Charles the European, the aristocrat, was the reincarnation of a knight from the High Middle Ages. She felt he emitted a mixture of smells from the pungent sap of the trees in France's forests. The soil of Charles's country did not have the same nuances of brown as the soil of the American northeast when it was not covered with snow. The soil of an Ile-de-France underbrush was lighter, more reddish, Charles de Roquemont had said. And Esther, during their walks around Norwich, dreamed of these tree trunks, these bare branches that the light from the winter sky, west of Europe, would turn sometimes almost red, Charles whispered to Esther, his eyes vibrant with abnormal passion. . . .

"I don't know why I'm so afraid," Olga said to herself.

"Charles who?"

"De Roquemont."

The man. Finally. The real one. Olga had looked for him in other men without ever finding him. And now he was standing before her; he was undressing her with his eyes. Her legs go limp. She is shaking convulsively. The two of them go on discovering each other, recognizing each other, indefinitely. He is the one. He is really the one. This face so irresistibly handsome. His blue, gold-flecked eyes. This mystery of death silently haunting life. He looks her over with his crazed eyes. . . .

"It has been years since I have been inhabited by a living man, a living woman," Charles whispers to Olga in a low voice, as if wanting to enter not through Olga's ears but through her belly, through her mouth, through her skin as she shivers, feels herself suddenly too alive, too tempting. . . .

How can one measure the dryness, the harshness hidden by a face, by the mucus membranes of a mouth, by the nails of a hand, by all the erotic surfaces that keep us from discovering the mind's hatred hidden away in the heart? Charles, hatefully, calculates. Olga's gaze rests admiringly on the man's pale cheeks, his fleshy, sinuous lips, his long, white fingers. He guesses her need for love, attention. This woman will be capable of giving her thoughts, her feelings, her life over to the other. There is much to receive from her, much to take from her. . . .

What is lacking in him abounds in her. No distrust on her part will block this man's reaching toward the north of being, toward the cold regions, the nowhere lands that he will reveal to her, will make her discover. The crazed masses will take root behind her eyebrows, behind her eyes, behind her forehead, inside her head; she will no longer be able to think, to defend herself; she will be contaminated; he will invade her. Just what is madness? Does this man contain traces of it? His eyes are too shiny, too fixed. Are there nothing but white, bare walls within his body, his brain?

Would there be no signs left of objects, of images, and would he resolutely get from her what he needs to see, to touch, because, for a long time, he has been barren? And he says, "I'm not very verbal. I hope that my silence does not bore you."

How many minutes, hours, or nights maybe, have they been facing each other? At first he was excited, talkative. Now, he is silent.

"It's not easy to produce waste, nothing but waste. It's like giving birth to dead children."

"I write life. A film script must make the characters come alive."

"Words. . . . But it's never alive, a word. It's a word. Nothing more."

He makes a face. Just what is madness? A world without words, a world that deprives us of meaning. He repeats to the scriptwriter, "In a six-hundred-page novel I have cut out all the book's chapter openings. That is, sixty thousand words, which I pasted on calling cards. I mounted the cards on little sticks. I planted the little sticks on a large white surface. A real paper scene. It took me two years to achieve this task of cutting and pasting. I, too, write, but it's a totally different type of writing. The text is made up of pasting and cutting. It's action. I touched sixty thousand words with my ink-stained knife. My writing is purely physical."

"Which novelist did you choose?"

"Fyodor Dostoyevsky. In an English translation."

"Why English?"

"I was in the United States."

"You brought your work back to France?"

"It's on exhibit in a Philadelphia museum. Over there, I'd work for up to eight or ten hours a day. I'd cut the pages up to let the right amount of light come through for each perforated word."

"What about the plot, the hero, the adventures?"

"It's the infinity of light. Cutting rewrites it."

Olga examines the dilated pupils. She has a strange faith in him. She loves this man's madness, whatever makes these eyes sparkle wildly. Somewhere, she understands him. She follows him. There should be no more meaning. There must be words only. She will not speak; she will ask nothing; she will not fault him for anything; they will no longer need words. He wants it so. Above the mouth, Charles's eyes are too shiny. Maybe, there, in front of him, Olga is like the aspens, the populars which, in certain latitudes, are choked by other species of trees, and maybe Olga, faced with Charles's madness, is like those thousand-year-old aspen groves that, little by little, are taken over by the spruce trees, by the fir trees within the vast, dark blue forests, in faraway regions, amid the boreal vegetation, up north, way up north of being, where it is colder, where there is less daylight. Olga is ashamed of her desire.

He tells her, "You're alive. I miss life. Life seeps out of me. . . . Let's be silent! Let's return to the body. For me, it's urgent. I need to feel, only feel. . . . Not speak."

The scriptwriter whispers in a hoarse voice, "Me too, I need to feel. I need what words can't give me."

Charles continues, turned inward as toward an abyss, "I only want to love. . . . Maybe I can love you. . . ."

"Love me?"

He looks straight into her eyes. "I love you."

Olga is stunned. "Me too."

He continues to look into her eyes and commands, "I want your smile, your softness, your sensuality. . . ." She can feel his breath upon her as he says, "I want your pussy. . . ." And as though he were talking to himself, "Discussions, sentences, this verbiage between people, I cannot stand it. It's life that I want to hear, to have wash over me like the waves of the rising tide; I want to lose myself in your hair, in your flesh. Olga . . ."

Burning hot, she flinches. "What you're telling me, those are still words. . . ."

"No, it's my hands gliding over you; can't you feel them?"

Olga fidgets on the bench. She wishes she were free to remove her suit jacket, her blouse. To be naked under the words that feel to the touch the way the ones she writes do; these words are no longer words because they come from the flesh to be read only by the flesh. Better than anyone, better than any woman, Olga absorbs this mad language that no longer has access to any symbol, this raw, direct language that's designed for the skin. . . . To see, only. To touch, only. She wants neither to understand nor to know; she wants nothing to do with intelligence, only with instincts. . . . The man's eyes shine, feverish. He kisses her.

It is dangerous to meet a werewolf. To spark life only to answer it with death. To create a presence the better to endure an absence, is that sadism? Is that impotence? To make a woman conscious that her belly, her breasts, her thighs are deprived of their own vibrations, of their own palpitations if this woman is not completed by the man. Manipulation of her being makes a woman aware of her incompleteness, of her dependence. Therefore a woman no longer exists without a man; a woman cannot be sufficient unto herself; therefore a woman no longer has a body without the body of a man; therefore a woman asks a man for life, another life; therefore, without him, she is only the living dead; therefore, in her need, lacking a man, she drags herself, she has cramps, her whole flesh aches, her organism slows down, unresigned to this decrease in vital energy. Therefore her mind grows dark. A woman is prone to depression. A man becomes her savior; he assumes the power. And a woman, defeated, intoxicated, will venerate him as he penetrates her and he restores this warmth and this movement that he would have made her lose by depreciating the strength of this woman who will no longer believe in anything but him, the other, as though, were he absent, she would have no more blood in her veins,

no more oxygen, no more air to breathe, as though she were suffocating. . . . That is how bewitchment is born. . . . Charles was
bewitching Olga. Charles was slowly putting Olga to death. Charles
liked to feel a woman come, reach orgasm, then collapse, panting, to
feel her being think of nothing but retrieving through him the blinding
intensity which seemed that much more precious, rare, because it was
given out sparingly by this man who, an enemy of women, liked to
watch their tired faces, read their deep thoughts, their solitude. After a
long period of abstinence, he would rush toward them, but only when
they were sexually desperate, when their nerves were almost sick
from feeling empty, gaping, too vibrant, and they were crying for no
reason, accusing the man without telling him why, without daring to
admit that their unfulfilled desires were consuming them, were foster-
ing this excitement that drives a woman crazy if the tension is not
released in pleasure and orgasm. Therefore at the last moment, when
the shattered victim was exhausted from sensuality, from agony and
from shame, when she was writhing, prey to the pangs of her sexual
yearnings, Charles, condescending, would dole out love, that drug
which can reduce the frustrated to animals. And Charles would
remark with surprise, "They're certainly bestial! What's happened to
their minds, to their dignity? No wonder we call them hysterics. . . ."
The smarter ones, or the least in love, had soon departed. He gives
Olga a long kiss. Only Esther had understood. But she had paid with
her life for her lucidity. One day, in Norwich, she had allowed Charles
to try on one of her evening gowns. Charles, dressed in the ball gown
of black and white taffeta ruffles, had admired himself in the mirror.
That night, in Esther's arms, he had never been more in love. Back in
France, alone in his apartment, he would imitate Esther's speech
habits, her high-pitched voice. He would also mimic other women,
especially old ladies.

Oh! this scent mixed with snow, frost, and hay fields . . . the
American scent of cold ground . . . how can one forget it? Charles
began to cry again.

"You're crying?" inquires Olga.

Oh! the scent of all these feelings which froze! which are cracked,
which no longer circulate, over there, through the morning air,
through the high currents flying above the forests, the lichen, in the
spring, when the snows are melting. . . .

Once more it is necessary to steer clear of him. He cannot stand this
void, this fixity anymore. He wants to live. He is going to have to steal
life . . . right where it is. . . . He is going to have to tear his prey to
pieces. Long ago the wolf used to pounce on man and his flocks, used
to disembowel his ewes. Charles is a maniac who, after a passionate

encounter, leaves behind a devastated and dying woman. In the old days peasants used to believe that striking a werewolf between the eyes with a pitchfork would make him regain his human form, that of a bedeviled, metamorphosed sorcerer, or of a demented man who was imagining he had been changed into a wild animal. In the bedroom, Charles used to like to release this savagery on Esther and, during lovemaking, he would debase the American; he would ask her to walk on all fours, to howl. The more he debased her, the more she would arouse his senses, the more heartily he would eat of her flesh, of her mouth. If Charles had been stripped, it would have been obvious that underneath there was the hide of the wolf into which he would once more be turned during this sadistic violence inflamed by love. . . .

Was Olga also going to be, after Esther, the regions that Charles, in his fear of women, knew how to conquer in order to terrify female bodies, hearts? Charles feels as though he were spying on himself; his memory is black and white. It is an X ray revealing his skeleton. In this black and white setting, from time to time Charles glimpses a multitude of tiny colored lights, resembling flickering specks which he would like to follow all the way to the colors of the flesh and of the clothes Esther wore the day of her death. This woman comes back to upset him in this French park as though she were not dead. Through dark-haired Olga, Charles can see the very blonde Esther. With the breath of a no longer breathing woman, Esther animates this live woman whom Charles will never be able to love, will never embrace as if she were Esther, because, in Artabassa, Charles killed Esther. . . . Thoughts flood over him. He cannot defend himself against the attacks of remorse. No one suspects him. The murderer was never found. In Charles's eyes Olga is blurred by his vision of Esther. The green eyes light up, enlarge the brown eyes. It is like the same woman with a double face. Like the face of a woman haloed by the face of another woman. There is something of the fantastic in all this. Is he kissing Olga? or Esther?

Does the son who has loved her too much ever kill his mother? She reappears in all women. Between any woman and the imprisoned son, this mother's magnetism is interposed. The son cannot be a man. The ghost stops the son's lips coming near the lips of the woman. The son turns away from the kiss. He turns away from the embrace; he wants to love only her. Charles frees himself from Olga's arms.

He killed her. He could still see the glassy eyes, Esther's hanging tongue. He thought he had once and for all gotten rid of the octopus that would not let go of him. He had pressed hard against the neck of the young woman who had been unable to cry out. But Esther, more seductive than ever, blonder than before, more perfumed, more

sensual, reappeared. Attracted by dark-haired Olga, by her Mediter-
ranean look, Charles, perhaps on the threshold of a new love, recognizes this reserve that takes hold of him and immobilizes him before a
woman, and he does not dare to speak another word, does not dare
make another gesture toward Olga, he does not dare take her hand or
smile at her again. Olga tenses up.

She will get the best of this reticent man's inhibitions, hesitations.
Having descended together into the wordless, lawless hell that he
promises her, they will voluptuously wrap themselves up into each
other, freed from all past ties. To lose language, to lose words, not to
speak anymore, is that not also to lose one's memory, one's origins, to
be reborn?

And then no one, no traces within you, will prevent you from rushing
toward the other. Olga is in a hurry. It is urgent for her to live, to live
her life intensely, quickly, to make up for lost time. When death is so
close, doesn't our instinct for survival become sharper?

To want to make up all at once for the life we have poorly lived, that
we have not appreciated, might be a prescient reflex when someone
dangerous takes possession of us. . . . The more life is taken from us,
the more we cling to what is still alive within us. . . . Olga is panting.
He is slipping away.

"Let's meet again tomorrow night. We'll have dinner at my house.
I'll show you my work."

The night conceals everything now, shapes, contours. Only
Charles's profile is traced by a white lunar line, the reflection of a
cloud. In this long nose, this high brow, this willful chin, is Olga
questioning the enigmatic profile of her fate? Should she back away?
This man does not look quite right. Who do we meet in parks on
summer evenings? Wanderers, voyeurs? All sorts of psychosexual
disorders. Even a madman who has killed his mistress thinking he was
killing his mother. Not for a moment is Olga aware of this drama. This
man is rather handsome; he is slender, something of a thoroughbred.
But before him, without knowing why, Olga feels ugly, outclassed,
desperate . . . obscurely so. Isn't there an aftertaste of death in the
strange new lease on life this stranger is inspiring in her? When desire
takes hold of us, which pole in us is reached? Does our inexplicable
nervousness already reveal to us the murderer who will make us his
next victim? What fatal need prompts people to suffer, to willingly
suffer so much, to want desperately to live, oh! to live again in vain?

Was Charles somewhat effeminate? Some of his facial hair was
missing; the lines of his face were too fine; his skin was too white, but
so soft. . . . His gestures were graceful. His erect penis would be
shocking, seem too big, too heavy, as though it conformed to laws that

defied biology. Virility with a powerful charm issued fleetingly from the mysterious femininity of this man. A little like a promise—that of giving what is not found in any specific gender. That of searching endlessly through the hybrid adventure of the union of the body with the imaginary. A promise which could only promise, remain incomplete, in rough form, know sensuality, sexuality outside of all norms. Never again to leave childhood, never to leave fantasy. To forget that we are depressed. Charles, from behind his too-long hair, from behind his feminine eyelashes, was hypnotizing Olga, who was finding in this lanky and bony silhouette of a used-up adolescent an aggressive and determined eroticism, one characteristic of last chances, the omnipotent will to live that replaces any corpse with a new living being.

Olga would flee in time from the business deals, the agents, the directors, the producers who were dipping into her blood, into her heart for the words for their popular movies, for the words of life, the drives, the surges, the warmth, the passion that the scriptwriter suddenly did not feel like giving to the movie but to this madman, this strange seer of this woman's forbidden feelings. Maybe he was an artist of raw humanity. For Olga, Charles had the colors of a distant territory. He was a deep valley, the torrential flow of a river carrying sand sequined in gold, gulches hollowed out in the limestone and the schist of a golden mountain, the tributaries of a great river sprinkled with islands and islets, flowing between rocky walls. This man must be coming back from far away.

He is arousing her.

⸢9⸣

From Mount Washington there was a view of rivers cleaved by waterfalls, of Appalachian mountain highlands whose lakes shimmered in the sun, of the Green Mountains, the White Mountains, near the Atlantic Ocean, covered with grazing land and forests. Charles, sensitive to the beauties of nature, had always marveled at America's scenic vastness, at the buildings painted red on the American farms lost in the middle of fields, at the spruce trees, the larch trees, the maple trees, the oak trees, the elm trees that lined freeways twice as wide as those in France. Charles did not differentiate between Esther and the Appalachian region that spreads, in North America, from Alabama to the Canadian border. For him the zones of conifers and broad-leaved trees and Esther, whom he felt to be foresty, cloudy, fluvial, were one and the same, a great sky, a wide region restoring the breath of life to Charles, regenerating him.... Now, right now ... this Olga ... in the night of this Parisian park ... the facets of a shattered mirror's pieces.

What is the use of attempting to renew contact with a dead woman through a live woman? Charles's chest and belly contract. Bloody knolls emerge from the debris, from the pile of images the murder left behind in the memories stratified in layers of red, violet, mauve, rose heaps, alluvial deposits of viscera from the hilly mental regions which nothing, no woman, will ever be able to level again. Esther forever lies disemboweled, torn into little gooey pieces. With his greyish blue, gold-flecked eyes, he probes Olga's fragile, almost tragic expression; he is going to enjoy tormenting this woman. Olga attempts a smile. What matters to Charles is this sudden flash of light, between his interior night and his exterior night; it is this rushing light which tears him away from himself and propels him toward someone, links him to someone. Charles is anxious to move, to renounce his inactivity.

Something is breaking in this man; he can hear the inner enclosure that fenced him in come crashing down. He aches horribly; the enclosure snapped. He is going to be able to see far away; he is going to be able to see a woman, to see the other. They are going to be able to meet. He is very near Olga. Just a few more steps. But will she ever make him free? Will he ever be free of the other? What power will a woman have over a man who thinks only of eliminating, of blotting out all women?

"Where are your works?"

The voice is confused. There are how many women? Which one is here? Which one is not? This Olga, this Parisian, is she a real woman?

"Hidden in museums, stored in basements or overseas . . . I can't remember."

It is like a mass deep inside you. It is shapeless, unnameable. It is not even a woman . . . it is no woman at all; it does not have genitals for the man; it does not have breasts for the man; it has never kissed you on the mouth; the penetration is insidious, it is . . . oh, yes! how to get rid of it? It is heavy like the belly of a female who is perpetually pregnant; it carries you; you do your best to hide; it is still in you; she never lets you go; she imprisons your fibers, your nerves; she is the one who comes back to get you started again if you try to forget her. . . . Not even alcohol can help; you are no longer sure of yourself, you no longer know who you are, she expulses you, your gender is doubtful, you have not been properly disconnected from her, there are still some feminine elements in the man that you are. You are tired of her holding you back for so long; you, who should have been her, not her be you; it was you, out of you that she made this miserable, effeminate wretch who, in spite of killing, massacring, will not find himself. Nothing is his, it is all hers; he belongs to her as though she had not let him be born, as though he were still being fed by her witch's blood, prolific, pregnant with a two-headed fetus, a double son, an androgyne . . . a mad artist.

˹10˺

Ever since this encounter, the inside of Olga's head has been ringing. She is nauseous, she is sick, she's looking for silence, they want to destroy her, she sobs, an implacable hatred is relentlessly pursuing her. Olga drinks tea to compensate for her other thirst. She empties the teapot. She is going to sleep no more but her overexcitement demands nourishment. Olga's body is as tense as a choleric, frustrated newborn which, the more it hears itself crying, the more it cries. It has to nurse. What is crying inside her is something organic, something alive, something torn out, oozing with blood. Between her and the pain, there is not a single thought, not a single word, as though the spirit did not yet exist, as though Olga could not yet speak to relieve her suffering, to unburden herself. . . . She is in the midst of basic, instinctive, impulsive matter; it is a life which is not yet flesh, only matter. There will be no release until the embrace which will give reassurance, will put an end to the anxiety, to this separation. Charles makes Olga hungry in order to make himself more indispensable. She is edging toward pure madness.

At one o'clock in the morning, Olga goes out in the street. She is crying. She buys some eye drops at the Saint-Germain Drugstore. Elderberry, cornflower, melilot, witch hazel, chamomile. . . . Each eye in its socket burns, stings. She speaks to the pharmacist.

"It's good for the eyes? It's natural? Those are plants? Just plants?"

The pharmacist has a calming effect. Olga relaxes at the sound of her soothing voice; the tone of a voice, even if it is impersonal, can, for a few minutes, have the generosity of a loving mother, can reach into our retracted, forgotten layers and temporarily comfort them.

What is the matter with her? Can a man, a madman, come near a woman in so physical a way and hurl her so far away from her own body, and drive her back to the origin of the body? To the origin of the earth? Give her back the most remote manifestations of life? As though jolted by a return to the stickiness of the womb, of the symbiosis that social constraints have subdued with such difficulty? As though we were suddenly losing our mind? As though we no longer knew anything? As though we were afraid of being once again nothing more than spasms, contractions, nothing more than muscular, fibrous movements which needed to cling to softness, to warmth? Childishly. There comes a time, just a few steps from the body, when obstructions and barriers disappear. Time no longer means anything; the primordial, mythical unit is created again; a man can be God for a woman. Therefore a woman will prostrate herself, humiliate herself, will beg. The man will rule over her, with all his law, with all his pride. And as for her, in this life which he will dominate, she will damage herself. Thus mastery determines virility, thus the power struggle was being established between Charles and Olga. . . . In order to avoid being a slave to flesh, the man wanted to be its master. But Olga thought that she would let herself be ruled by her flesh, her skin, her pussy; she was acquiescent.

If she had been Charles, Olga would have telephoned an Olga that he would have passionately loved; he would have poured out his feelings in the middle of the night in a verbal torrent of desire, to announce that he was rushing over, that he could no longer control himself, that he needed to envelop her, be one with her. But Charles, on the other side of life, was waiting. He had learned to restrain himself, to watch himself, to kill off those too emotional parts of himself. Because the less alive we are, the less we suffer. Suffering, which he wanted to avoid, had turned this mad killer into a cold, stony man, all the more attractive for not being attracted. Eyes closed, the victim would rush toward this deathly caress. Like Esther, Olga would be writhing under the sensuality which to her would have the sneer with which she guessed Charles would greet her when Olga would come to undress, to lie down, to offer herself, to grovel at the foot of this stranger's bed, on the wood floor, when she would no longer be able to endure being kept at a distance. . . .

After a few days, prudish Olga had reached that state which any decent woman restrains herself from ever reaching and to which any respectful and tender man is careful not to bring the one he loves. . . . But it was possible to make a sacrificial animal out of her. It is permissible to kill animals, not humans. And to dare kill, we would no longer need to see before us the human being; we would need to see only blood, only meat and a lacrimal liquid if she is crying, otherwise we would feel sorry, we would spare her, we would understand the futility of our resentment and maybe then the one we were ready to slaughter would elevate us to love. Maybe the act of profanation could be converted into an act of sacralization because, as we view the animal, our animality rises to the surface where we are as near to sin as to innocence, and we would then fall to our knees before this woman. We need to expiate, we need to feel forgiven because the divine is never far from earth, behind our acts whose baseness is outlined like the night's clouds against the immensity of the sky. . . .

⸢11⸥

Between that evening when he invited her to come to dinner at his house the next day and now in the damp street in the Sixth Arrondissement where, intoxicated with anticipation, Olga is running, in the Parisian summer, holding tight against her chest the collyrium for her irritated eyes, how many hours have tormented Olga? How many days, nights? Charles has not telephoned. She does not know his address; she does not have his telephone number; therefore she will not even have the occasion to debase herself while wandering and hanging round outside apartment buildings, to resign herself to going up to the door and ringing the bell hysterically until he opens. If she is possessed, it is not by desire, even less by love, but by an uncontrollable necessity to go to the ends of dependence and need. . . . Femininity is producing its drug in this woman's senses like the shadow that death persistently throws over our enlightened zones, inside our bodies shaken with darkness, which propels us toward our destiny that this live woman named Olga Vassilieff, like all earthlings, will fulfill. She is walking down the Boulevard Saint-Germain; she is dragging her feet, exhausted by insomnia. Then she runs, she jumps, she leaps toward the stranger outlined by bright lights, with sparkling, flickering flashes inside the darkness of her mind.

She no longer has a choice. Her life is reaching the moment of reckoning. It will be necessary to pay with the body what Olga has continually been putting off until a later date. Time is a judge that, at the expiration date, forces us to pay our debt. And on some summer evening, in a park, he dispatches toward us a representative of his law. And then we must yield, even if we must die; we no longer have a choice. The scene takes place under the dusty trees of Paris; and it is the electricity of our body which, facing the demonic angel, has warned us: this lightning flash is the time for love.

⌐12⌐

Eyes fixed on the ground, he was not saying anything. Olga was standing right in front of him. She was no longer dark-haired but blonde; she was the other one. The necrophiliac was racked with fever. In New York, Esther had stood out among the other female guests the night of the exhibit when Charles had asked a painter to introduce him to this extraordinary blonde.

"Am I disturbing you?"

The room was large, with high ceilings. There were no windows.

"No, come in; I was working. . . ."

He had finally called her. Olga was looking at him. He appeared distraught but his patience was intact. Dirty cups were stacked up on top of dictionaries and encyclopedias with torn covers. Olga, embarrassed, was examining the visual precision with which he seemed to be staring at her from head to foot.

"Here, I live with no one. I need to be alone, totally alone, to create."

After a moment of bewilderment, Olga gradually became more cheerful. She began to sit down.

"Take a cushion, it won't be as hard as the tile floor. . . . Do you want some coffee?"

"No . . . tea, if you have some. . . ."

There was a clap of thunder. Rain was pouring down.

"I'm meticulous, an ultraperfectionist; I might be a little bit fanatical; I avoid the fashionable. When my friends see me turn my back on international exhibits to spend eight, ten hours a day cooped up in this room, they think I'm an idiot. I'm a contemplative man; I have to have my walls, my tiles, my ceiling to look at. Sometimes sunshine showers my desk. . . ."

She noticed the desk: an architect's table.

"Your name's Olga Vassilieff and you write . . ."

"This film script that I'll novelize later."

" 'Novelize'?"

"I will write a novel from the film script."

He exclaimed, "Writing! Words scratched on paper! The ideal contraption for communicating urges. . . ."

He was speaking mechanically. His head ached. He was quoting, " 'I've made many outer journeys, now I am making inner journeys. . . . I like staying cloistered at home. . . .'

"I have soundproofed the room. Nothing from the outside reaches me. Whether it's two in the morning or two in the afternoon, it's the same. . . . Outdoors, life is waiting for me, calling me, the trees, the park. . . . But it's been this way for five years; I'm indoors, I'm a hermit. . . . I wanted my walls white and bare, no pictures to distract my thoughts. People in the visual arts accuse me of being too abstract. Maybe I should take some time to rest. I've been putting up with this damned fatigue for five years; off and on my blood pressure drops. To tell the truth, talking nonstop to someone the way I did to you the other evening, in the park, relaxes me; it soothes something in me. Because otherwise, sometimes, in my solitude, I have the feeling that my work is absurd, producing nothing more than dead thoughts."

He lay down flat on the floor; he buries his face in a red cushion; she is afraid he might begin sobbing as he did that first day, in Monceau Park. He stands up; he takes long strides across the studio; he waves his hands about, moans in a strangely feminine voice. He suddenly has a slight American accent that she had not noticed before.

"After all, I publish tourist brochures of a country that no longer exists, the traces, the witnesses . . ."

"Witnesses to what?"

He pierced her with a glance.

What he would not give to escape from this deathly dust, the bushes in the park watching him as soon as he goes out. How can he escape the power of objects and places? Succeed in having everything stand still? So that he will not be filled with disgust?

He has come closer to her, his eyes more feverish.

"You have a fabulous life inside you. I'm going to love you; I can sense magnificent things lie ahead for you."

Olga backs away. He continues, "Where are we, you and me? You, you're over there, me, I'm over here. . . . You're over there, aren't you? Over there?"

She does not understand. "Over there?"

He can no longer make her out; he is very near her but he is far away; he is only absence. He whispers, "It's as crazy as having a swimming pool that's always empty. . . ."

Through the window (but there is no more window; there is no more reality), a menacing star continually targets him with its bluish sparkle, near the moon rippling with the light reflected from the ocean. . . . This man inhabits his brain, nothing but his brain. . . .

"Ever since my return, my friends say I've changed, that I'm more secretive than usual. They say there's a presence inhabiting me. Do *you* think there's a presence inhabiting me?"

His eyes are flashing with hatred. A long Inuit chant about white wolves in love with the sparkle in the snow and the ice. . . .

"I'm speaking to you as though there were a disease in my family. I must be unhinged because of all those lacelike pages that I cut out day in and day out for my 1989 exhibit of two thousand slashed pages. I'm working on a futile project. Like corpses on a battlefield, my work will only serve to feed the vultures. I haven't been interested in it for years; nothing interests me anymore. The other evening, seeing you in the park, I suddenly felt a great need for fresh air, for life. I need you. Before meeting you, I'd do everything I could to disappear, to slip into oblivion. My art seemed to be that of another man who was dying . . . it had a taste of mourning. . . . I'm going to take you to stationery stores. Do you like to spend hours looking at paper?"

He stares at her intensely with the crazed eyes of a maniac. Olga Vassilieff is afraid. For this man, words are no longer words; they are reduced to sounds that can be seen, touched, but whose meaning has been lost, has been stifled. He will silence their meaning. Always. We will never know. We will never know if it is alive or has stopped living. He will keep quiet. He will have rendered the French tongue mute. The American tongue too. . . . He would like to hear Esther speak.

On the other side of walls, summer forms deposits, like green sand, on the tree limbs drenched by the rain shower.

"I no longer need to travel. Before, I used to go to America. I used to go to Vancouver. It's always raining out there. I used to go to the Rockies. I used to go to Milwaukee. Now, I don't go anywhere. I'm in a foreign country inside myself. Don't you ever feel as though everything is going to destroy us? Time, of course, but also space?"

He is about to pour his heart out. His confession is about to gush out like the sweat beading on his forehead, under strands of hair.

"Day after day, lacerating the pages of a book with a razor blade so I can isolate words and paste them on cardboard, do you think that's creating? It's impotence, that's what it is. My agents, gallery managers, art magazine critics absolutely love what I do but these works are an imposture; they compel me to sign contracts with arrogant retailers who think they'll be able to ask me to lick their boots. Working seventeen months to exhibit for twenty days a setup which will be taken down in two hours, that's the opposite of a masterpiece which defies eternity. . . ."

His insides have been screaming for years. It is like the music of the wind we hear outside, a music that snaps off limbs, uproots trees. Mad cursive writing twirls, especially at night, through his ears, through his eyes. He no longer sees the lines on the pages of the novels he cuts up. These words of various shapes merge amid the rumblings of men, animals, women, children—keep him awake, pursue him, accuse him.

The racket mixes everything in a jumble of signs. Charles's vision is blurry; he sees double. It is all staggering, deafening; his brain is being crushed. He would like to run away, go back over there.

But if this Olga does not slip away, blood will return to Charles's veins, a new blood; it will be the end of the unbearable symphony which for five years has been extoling in slow tempo dying Esther's martyrdom. These cacophonies still stick to his hands, his eyes, his skin, to the distorted senses of a murderer who seeks in vain to kill, kill, and kill again, for all eternity. . . .

At his worktable, the vandalizing artist was finally getting the best of the unnameable; he was furiously working on each word, on writing, on life, on spoken words; he was eliminating; he was shredding; he was bearing down hard to make holes in the printed paper; the words had to become illegible again, invisible like those of his secret guilt.

Olga recoils before the model of this delirious work, this cemetery of words angrily taken from the pages of a book. Arranged in alphabetical order, the words are filed on toothpicks. Immolated language is buried there.

"Here is every single word of my native tongue. . . ."

She thinks, He's mad . . . he's mad. . . .

This mausoleum is the product of a sick mind. Only Charles knows the meaning of this imaginary death. Olga, ill at ease, asks for some tea. Inwardly the scriptwriter is revolted by this charnel house of ink and cardboard. Now Dostoyevsky's novel is nothing more than repeated rows of words without sentences, nothing more than the graveyard of literature that has been cut to pieces, ground up by savagery. Nothing identifiable must survive. What is Charles hiding? What does he want to hide from himself? Why methodically rip up rules, etymologies, definitions, by sabotaging a language's operation; why retain from this translation only a fleshless skeleton that will never speak again?

"I was inspired by pop art, by the plastics and post-automatist trends, by the happenings movement," Charles answers Olga's suspicious eyes.

From very far away she hears the lunacy of the words estranged from their meaning. Charles continues, pedantically, "Conceptual art, kinetic and generative art, video art, artistic decompartmentalization, multidisciplinary experiments, the International Symposium on Sculpture all helped me reevaluate theories and schools and initiate a different reading of reality, as all performing artists do who have in common a desire to appropriate nonsense."

The murderer explains, "Performance does not exist outside of the act and it does not manifest itself in an object."

Olga, heart racing, lets herself be penetrated, in half-tones, in half-words, by this annihilation of language for which another language is substituted, disquieting, close to the liver, the belly, the crotch, the breasts, the lungs, the throat, the vulnerable, excitable, and defenseless parts of the flesh. She senses the stubborn furor of this man.

He can feel sadism invading him again. Charles will hastily leave the south, will proceed toward the north, toward this linguistic desert, toward these silent territories cleared of all vocabulary; he will have access to the outermost bounds of himself; in the untamed north, he will once more travel over lakes, frozen bays, millions of rivers and tributaries, millions of waterfalls; once more he will head for spaces which nothing can fill, for a hardened stream. Once again, fear deep down in his guts, once again, an insatiable hunger, once again, to be convulsed with pain, once again to be taken by her, by this inexplicable woman, by the impossibility of loving, once again the insurmountable excess of madness's climatic, geographic surfaces, once again, this revenge, this impotence, once again fantasy ripe for drilling, exploiting, prospecting, extracting the sour sap of hate, once again the threat of disintegration, once again these intimate subregions, these deserts, Eagle Plain, these shivering jungles of horror where, hidden away, unaware, behind a smile, behind seductive tenderness, we are on the lookout, foundations are laid bare; once again, the hundreds of millions of years of the age of anxiety, once again to go back inside her, to travel through her cliffs, her taiga, her tundra, the icy feeling of no longer being alive, once again to rake one's own flesh like a field of ice strewn with forbidding rocks, once again the stone wall, once again, the town that is too big, too empty, once again, he feels alone.

⌐13⌐

Olga would like to murmur, "Take me, here, now. Take me, don't make me wait anymore." Outside the night is warm. . . . Not wait anymore. . . . Because of their thick foliage, the trees in the park dim the light from the lampposts above the bench. Does Charles want the body of this woman? Or does he wish for something more, such as her spirit, her thoughts; does he wish to dominate this woman's personality, take it away from her so that she will be reduced to raw nerves, flesh, instincts, reflexes, deprive her of any power over her own will, completely reduce a woman's existence so she will lose her head, seduce her, enslave her atoms, her cells, be superior to her? Olga will soon be no more than leg, thigh, breast spasms, baited expectation. He is firm. He caresses her. She feels faint. She wishes he would be more daring. It's not easy on this bench. A voyeur might be spying on them right this moment. Charles's spirit is sick with the need to steal this woman from herself. To kill the body, it is first necessary to kill the spirit, before starting on the skin, the organs and therefore succeed in denying this hated femininity and Charles continues. . . . His masculine hands spark the flame, the clitoris, "Let's go to your house," she says, "this isn't a good place, someone could see us. . . ." Did Charles hear? But then she cries out the opposite, "I want, now, here, right away, I can't stand it anymore. . . ."

Her body is imploring. But the impotence that has taken hold of Charles is self-inflicted; Charles enjoys being unable to satisfy this female in heat; he enjoys seeing her humanity being degraded; she struggles, too passive, too sensual, to preserve her dignity. Olga begins to sob. "A fit of hysterics," Charles notices. She is on fire, totally on fire. It is as though Charles's fingers and tongue were flames devouring her. He tells her, "I want to lick you."

She goes rigid, her body arched.

"I want to go inside your belly," he whispers.

The fire spreads through her; this man's mouth speaks to her right up close, almost in her flesh, "Don't you think that you and I, that we're going to experience something that our bodies have never known?"

She is his; she has nothing left untouched. Everything in her is clogged with desire; she is a scrap of physiological body disfigured, congested by insatiability, by sexual obsession. Charles's spirit penetrates Olga, slowly, very slowly, with greed, while she feels as though she is dying like an animal.

Once back home, a pain in the lower abdomen will make her double over. How can she free herself, by herself? Someone is playing with her excitability, with her sexuality. Olga, too feminine, does not know how to defend herself. She wishes she were frigid. Oh! if only she were no longer alive! If she were not so alive anymore! Would he get as much pleasure from killing her? He asks, icily, politely, "Would you like to look for a little hotel?"

She says in the voice of a little girl, shyly, "Why not go to my place?"

Charles thinks a while. He says that there is his single bed in his studio apartment but he does not dare offer it; it would be uncomfortable. Can't he realize the state he has got her in? Right now she would accept this man anywhere, on a kitchen table, on the tile floor, on a window ledge. She is desperate. Olga sees the god's penis rise. The man-god, above her, suddenly stands up straight in all his monumental height. It is absolute fantasy. Olga, in just a few days, has been transformed into a hysterical woman. Charles is jubilant; his eyes brighten. Panting, she is ready to beg, "again . . . again . . . farther . . . deeper. . . ." How vile they are! How bestial they are! How they make him sick! Pigs! He has always thought that of all women. Even Esther. He feels growing in him the loathing which inhibits his masculine behavior, his masculine feelings. He stops. He has known too many ejaculations without orgasm; no woman has known this; no woman will know this. Otherwise, how else can he continue to seduce them, to destroy them, to seek revenge on them? for this desire, for this pleasure which he gives them and which they do not give him? This joy of being a woman, no woman will reveal it to Charles, will make him woman. He hates women. He rejects them all. Oh! how he suffers from so much hate!

Two nights later:

"Charles!" Olga moans as he penetrates her, as he kneads her violently, as he lies down between her two fleshy, twitching thighs. "Oh! Charles!"

In the bedroom of a little hotel on Rue du Parc, she licks him; she sops him; she makes his penis sticky with her mouth. As for him, more than ever master of his hate, he is at work in the most remote corners, the least little networks of nerves and veins of this gaping woman. They are pagans, women without religion. Aren't they ashamed of idolizing a penis? The in-and-out rubs her, massages her. Aren't they ashamed of venerating nothing more than a sex organ? How despicable they are for having such a crude nature! The devil in her body, a fire up her ass, Charles's mother would say about his sister who had been sleeping with boys since she was twelve years old. "Is your sister the one who was fucked by the whole high school?" Charles, an adolescent, would blush. They have no affinity for spirituality; they do not know how to be ascetic, how to mortify their flesh. They groan with orgasmic pleasure the way a dog howls at death. God! how they nauseate him!

14

Charles, distraught with remorse, remembered the nocturnal rays, but almost nothing diurnal. The steel and glass musical sounds of the snowy city, the skyscrapers, the kisses, the mad and twirling city, the glass walls of the city pivoting on its sky-and-water axle when, in the Champlain Hotel elevator, he and Esther rose one floor at a time above the river, above the huge span of one of the longest rivers in the world, a city galactic with stars and chasms which they could look over from their hotel terrace, a city swarming with descendants of Greek, Jewish, English, French, Polish, Irish, Chinese, German, Russian immigrants who had built their community on a volcano and on land belonging to Sioux, Iroquois, Montagnais Indians, a city with distant Eskimo provinces, a city of water sprites, dragons, eagles, jazz, and smoke, a city in a country whose west coast looks toward Japan, a city from which trappers and gold prospectors set out toward the inviolate north and west, a city of cocaine, aphrodisiacs, steamed hot dogs, beer, graffiti, bums, musicians, dancers. In winter its suburbs were surrounded by ski runs lighted all night long, by slopes livid with snow, and then there were the forests and the roads which, gigantic in size, rivaled its river. Afloat on its river, the island city, the iceberg city illuminated it with its streetlights and its beacons from one bank to the other, from one bridge to the other, among cranes, bulldozers, construction sites, trucks, barracks, hospitals, taxis, taverns, universities animating this vast lunar skating rink, isolated from the rest of the world's traffic by ice floes. Before boarding the plane at Dorval Airport and taking off for Artabassa, Charles and Esther had spent a two-week hiatus between the two northern areas: one, still in the south, and the other in the farthest of northern blizzards and freezing fogs . . . white flurries in the blue and black night when Charles and Esther trampled through the icy mud, between the life they were going to leave behind and the death that is ahead of us. . . . Wrapped in her fur-lined coat and her layered shawls, her neck protected by fur boas she wrapped around her thin body entwined in beaver and black lynx, Esther was frozen with cold. She was slender, too elegant. She aroused him. He would shoot jealous glances in her direction. But Esther, clouded by the fierce charm of this man, was not conscious of Charles's hostility and, without hesitation, was giving in to the one she called her lost boy, her neurotic son.

"Where're we going?"

"Nowhere."

"Nowhere?"

She was passionately in love; she was mad about this cannibalistic dandy, his human flesh-eating and blood-drinking eroticism. The young Nosferatu, with the English rock-singer face, had taken Esther away from her prejudices, from her puritanism. For him, she was now no more than food and blood, flesh and blood, sex and death, woman all over her skin, woman all under her skin, in this descent into the depths of the self.

"I'm a bad boy," said the son of the night, "come with me."

Their snatches of words, in English or in French, were reduced to the rhythms of a funereal dance, the sounds of a requiem during which Esther would sometimes interrupt herself long enough to repeat, "Help me, please . . . you frighten me. . . ."

Drunk, he would wander outside. And she would be waiting for him in the hotel room, waking up every hour.

"Who's there?"

But he was still not back. And then finally, in the late hours . . . almost at dawn and she, her eyes rolled upwards, "Don't kill me. . . ."

He, in a soft voice . . . very soft . . . the softness of a mother singing a lullaby to her infant, would try to calm her, "You'll never die. . . ."

That night, he was using his madman voice, his killer-son voice, his son-sick-of-her voice, sick of the curse. Oh! sick as soon as he would love . . . as soon as he was driven mad by love returning to ambush him, to throw him off balance, to bring him closer to this gaping hole, to vertigo, at the end of this night, in front of this too feminine, too disarming woman, "Who's she? Who's she?"

He could not see her anymore, could not recognize her anymore, and, as though he wanted to comfort her for having hurt her until she collapsed, fainting from pain, before dying from a hemorrhage, "It's not too late for you," he would whisper to the closed eyes of this woman to whom he wanted to give the ultimate pleasure. . . .

He would listen to her dying. He would be one of the walking dead for the rest of his sadistic life. She must have had a premonition. Seated on the bed, her face contorted with fright, she had screamed at Charles, "I say: go away!"

But Charles was obeying orders other than those of life. He was kissing, biting, squashing Esther with his whole weight of energies suddenly unchained. His breath smelled of whiskey, beer; Esther was fighting back under him, "I don't want to . . . I don't want to . . . no . . . no. . . ." And weakening, "I want . . . I want. . . ."

What she was calling for, what for so long she had been calling for, finally, he was hearing it, without contradictions, without countermand, without adulteration; and he was giving it to her. God! how beautiful she was in her dress of blood, her dress glistening with flowing blood. . . . Never had she seemed so natural, so blonde. Never before had her skin looked so like the lights, the illuminations which can be seen reflected in the river, one of the longest in the world, when, upon arriving after miles and miles of forests in the northern United States, one approaches Montreal, a city rising out of the night, where Esther and Charles had stopped over before reaching Artabassa, fear, horror, at the end of these twirls, these swirls of frost, in their stomachs, in their flesh, in the anxiety which no longer had a human solution. . . .

Once again, hesitation, from one ocean to another, once again trying to find a gratification which will no longer respect rights, limits, once again tightening the hold on Esther as if she were a gold mine, once again virgin territory, its misty isles, its hail, its ice, its polar circle, ideas strewn with stones, stubborn arguments, this uncivilized region; once again Charles was this traveler lost in masculine violence; he was a pilgrim from the north in a world of desolation and fog, this pious believer in the nonexistence of God where criminals are relaxed, resting in blood and death; once again he was bent beneath heaps of mental snow; once again, a vagrant, he was getting deeper into the semi-arid prairies. It is possible to die of cold and misery, abandoned by all, and closed off from life's commerce as a river which, iced over, would flow north toward ever more ice. Charles froze; women paralyzed him.

"You torment me," he told Olga.

An unreal country replaces these real countries he has known; he no longer knows where he is, where he is returning from, if he is back; he might still be over there, stuck in her, in her marshes, in her icy waters, over there where one summer, she took him up Mount Dawn, to its flat ridges covered with short grass. Dead son still inside her, he would accompany her, follow her. Perhaps he was still there, attached to the viscera, which the windswept shores, coastal waters, and coves were only duplicating like a magnifying mirror, belonging to this giant whose shoals were red, a region whose outlines were steep with banks and mountains red with mucous membranes to which were appended obscene, gaping lips through which she was devouring him.

The weather was too beautiful; it was too hot; the sky was too blue. Olga Vassilieff was afraid to leave her house, to go to the park for some air; she was shutting herself away; she wanted to expel the sap that summer was breathing into her limbs made heavy with the inactivity which, in fear of her own body, she was imposing on herself now that she was on the verge of toppling into the ravine, this bottomless pit, this abyss which is, for a woman, her own feverishly gaping sexuality. To come . . . to feel. . . . She knew that outside it would be worse, as vegetal, as green or golden as fields, forests, lands buzzing with flowers and tufts populated with insects, in her feminine desire growing like a prepubescent little girl whose flat, boyish breasts swell under the rush of hormones and Olga was struggling against getting younger; she was mortifying her flesh; she was arresting her inner spasms of rebirth; she was fleeing from the sun; she was barricading herself behind her closed blinds; she unplugged the telephone; she was cutting herself off from the outside world; she was evicting from her thoughts the simple smell of grass, oh! to think of the smell of hay out in the surrounding countryside, the darkness of a barn, the flutter of a white butterfly's wing would have rekindled the very much alive woman in her; she would not have been able to stand the down feathers, the pollen, the tickling of the wind, the evening's iridescent mildews; the day, musty with the bluish leaves on the damp park shrubbery, would not spare her overexcited senses, too ready to obey the call of the soil scented by summer, amid the blaze of the city without exit. . . . This anxiety without exit, always without exit.

Would Olga see Charles today? Would she telephone him or would she spend another day waiting? Absurd to wait, since the telephone was unplugged. . . . Olga was going mad; within itself her body was spying on its veins, arteries, lymph glands, capillaries, grooved, smooth muscles, the anatomy of its heartbeats, prisoners of her fear to love Charles de Roquemont, to love him enough to suffer, to die.

Two or three nights a week, Charles would meet Olga in the park. Each time he swore to himself he would end it, would not go farther into this fantasy love affair; he no longer wanted to blot out Esther's ghost with Olga's body.

Was he pursuing a ghost, a body? or rather another frenzied attempt to see the invisible? A woman's invisible parts, her insides, her viscera, all that is visible only when she is dead, dissected, when the roundness of her breast, her belly, her hip, her buttock is cut to pieces, when her external contours are destroyed, the ones hiding the magnificent internal, uterine shapes to which a man penetrating her has access only through touch, never through vision, inside the naked woman as though it were forbidden to the eye, to any human eye, to any impious voyeurism to look at the caverns, the grottos, the great mucous rooms, site of the spasms of our conception that hungry, thirsty sexual desire ceaselessly licks, nibbles, rubs, pierces, blindly, to force its way, to climb back up the slope of life which, without help, conveys us toward death in our desperate curiosity.

Performance: 840 times, stab the softness, 864 times, amid the silence of a city asleep, in Artabassa asleep, impose silence on all this bodily softness. Let there be nothing left of Esther! nothing of her voice, nothing of her moans, nothing of her music! Charles has not eaten in fourteen hours. By the handful he extracts the insides; he pulls out the intestines, the glands. Esther is dripping, covered with blood. No doctor, no surgeon could save her now. It is too late. Her murderer has knifed her in the abdomen 864 times. It is too late. In one hour, instead of getting out his traveler's checks or his Visa card, he will pay cash for the room under an assumed name. Eighty dollars. No one at the front desk will be aware of the nightmare.

"My wife didn't sleep well; she's resting. She's not to be disturbed; I'll wait for her in the bar. . . ."

He is careful; he controls his voice, his movements. He is afraid of giving himself away. At the bar, he smokes one cigarette after another. Just a sign from him would expose the whole bloody truth. He cannot stop anymore. . . . If he could, he would begin again stabbing, counting, going beyond, 840, 874 . . . go to one thousand . . . the only way to calm down . . . one hour, seven hours more . . . to kill her longer . . . more fully. . . .

"Sir, what's the big idea of playing the same tune over and over?"

"I snapped . . . my brain tilted. I don't know when I started. . . ."

Women have often been compared to a musical instrument, a guitar, a violin, a piano. As for him, it is the piano he plays, a requiem; he is like a machine; it is automatic, one more run over the keyboard, a second run over the keyboard; he goes over the whole keyboard, all the notes, all the sounds, from the deepest to the highest, but no one has guessed; the cries are believed to be cries of pleasure. He tortures her out of pleasure; she yells out of pleasure; she is dying out of pleasure.

"You're happy?"

It was in Artabassa; it lasted seventeen hours. Seventeen hours of total happiness. No. Seventeen hours deep in winter and snow. Charles could sense the people, the neighbors, supportive of this nocturnal intensity. The hotel and the city were quiet. The knife, with zest, was celebrating the chilly night, the night of men from the cold region.

Charles watches Olga. Can any woman be anything other than redundant for him? He is always coming back to this aquatic and blood-soaked environment, this natal tonality, as though he had never become used to being out in the air, as though he were still in an embryonic state, fetal amid this unobstructed flow, in these women, this woman from whom he could not extricate himself and who was slowing down his life evolution, was keeping him from attaining adulthood, the tissue stage of healed skin where he would have had his own entity, where he would no longer have been her parasite, where he would no longer have been constantly pulled backwards in his fascination for the interior environment which he no longer wanted to leave. All he knew now was to split up, to bore into himself to infinity in this metamorphosis where, larvalike, he could reach the anterior regions; he was nothing more than connective tissues unattached to Esther, nothing more than this woman's ganglions; he could no longer tell the difference between himself and the blood vessels of any woman; he was in the circulatory, dermal, abdominal redness; he had only the beginnings of a muscle structure; his features were longitudinal, oblique, lateral, inside these segmentary women, inside these organs seen from too close up, inside Esther's, Olga's thickness where all women are identical, the very liquid where, pregnant, they are life at its beginnings. Charles was barely developing. He was limited to their genital cavities; he was not a whole person; he and these women shared organs. Charles was not autonomous. He did not have a distinct anatomy; he would not be able to survive if Esther were to expel him; he was at the mercy of a whole system; he was subject to the multiple interactions of love and hate in his perpetual self-division into pieces rooted in this female who would never end up destroying herself in the one who was fused to her, turned toward this softness which, although stabbed 848 times, retained the same tenderness, surrounded him with reminiscences, with fears. . . . For this son, was the need to be delivered a battle lost before it was begun?

Olga no longer went out for air or for light; she did not have the time; she would watch the days, the hours go by from the window of her bedroom where she waited at night for the moment when she would meet Charles in the back room of a café near the park.

"Sometimes plastic arts are a high. No need to sniff coke; you can invent fantastic stuff, drape the Palace of Versailles in rustling tulle so it looks like some Bolshoi ballerina."

Charles, exhausted, drained, would talk all night: "Heroin's for the lower classes; shooting up with heroin is cheaper. Coke, if you just take enough for a toot, is not a hard drug; it just gives you a feeling of power. Where do you find cocaine anyway? Where there's power and dough: movies, politics, journalism."

Everything seemed pointless to Olga; reality was pathetic. Writing a film script, writing a novel, how futile! Charles, half drunk, was teaching Olga the futility of her efforts: "People aren't into words; they're into pictures. The word is over. People are voyeurs. They have to imagine that they're touching, that they're fondling. But the blah-blah of words, they don't give a damn. Their minds are tired and your scripts, your stupid dialogues, that whole shitty literature that warps the picture and the sound, well the public doesn't give a crap. People want fucking, some ass, pricks, everything that they don't do, everything that they don't have because they're poor bastards. . . . Hypnosis, lots of fucking, lots of pricks. Because all your words, they make people vomit. There are too many words; we can't take any more of these words that don't mean anything anymore. We're in the middle of a word crisis, a word inflation. We don't have bodies anymore, all we have is speech. We talk, we talk, but we don't feel anything anymore; we're all impotent, asexual; we s & m each other sentences on end and we don't touch each other anymore; we don't kiss properly anymore; we don't know how to penetrate a woman anymore. Does a woman know how to make a man feel that she's a woman? that it's soft and warm to touch a woman, that it's good? that it smells good? that it smells like wheat, like blonde wheat? that it smells like hay, country roads, riverbanks, that what the body is missing is tenderness?"

Olga, moved, was listening to Charles, the other Charles, the one who, maybe one day, would be born of her. . . .

"Don't write anymore, Olga; words aren't going anywhere, even movie dialogue; they're words too. Before, the movies were silent and that was real cinema. Words don't reach people anymore; they have no more meaning; meaning is elsewhere. Look for it in your life, in your skin, in your flesh. There's only sexual joy to give meaning to the passing of time, day, night, seasons. Life is in the buttocks, in the thighs, in the mouth, in the ass. Life is elementary; life is not words, no; it's as elementary as the palm of the hand. Life's untamed; life's juicy."

"We aren't animals," says Olga, deep in thought, "there's civilization, taboos, we're not alone. . . ."

"On the contrary, we are alone. Alone with our desire and nothing else."

Charles, eyes gleaming, watches for animal life in her, in him. . . .

"It's because they unmask, unveil, that words bother you, right?" Olga asks softly.

For her and for him, there is no more destiny. It was as though Charles and Olga no longer wanted a destiny. Olga, guided by

Charles, was going backwards toward a return to her origins, to some primitive state. She was being dragged as if from behind herself. Within she could hear the words receding, regressing; she could hear them taking root in her flesh, in her drives. She was reaching a time before there was any law, identity, gender, naming. Everything was once again allowed: delay, fusion. Language was leaving the verbal behind. In spite of the pain, Olga had never felt so young, so new. . . . This woman and this man, were they, after all, nothing more than body, nothing more than sexuality; were they what precedes love, what precedes development? Neither she nor this man needed to name each other any longer; they were leaving our era; they were deserting our epoch; they no longer wanted any part of our technological ages; they wanted carnal times, nothing mechanical, nothing inhuman, nothing frigid. . . . Olga stubbornly believed Charles; she was trusting. He was right. In no time at all, our world of images would be able to do without writing, vocabulary, grammar; there would be no more language. Why do we continue using words? There would be no more books, no more dictionaries. So, yes, she wanted to become a child again, to feel small, as if time had not passed, as if there were still epics, novels immersed in the flesh and blood of the body damned by love and hate whose concluding sentences soon would announce a speech about to end, the bankruptcy of writers and poets. . . . Oh! to avoid seeing the end come. . . . Oh, to seek refuge in the most archaic past of words, in their origins, right where feelings keep us from thinking. . . . To refuse to face the future, progress, to refuse to face the fact that human life, all instinct and voice, all vibrant, emotional, was in the process of reducing itself to mathematics, to scientific formulas, to signs more abstract than words. Spontaneous life could no longer be communicated, would be repressed by an order which would judge it obscene. Olga, no longer able to disentangle madness from despair, felt ready to plunge once again into the cruelty, into the pain of this prehistory of our body where she was being led back by a retarded man, a sick man, a survivor of this barbarism that is hidden from us by our conscience and, suicidal, Olga was letting her guard down with Charles in a muted violence.

Seated at the terrace of the park café, facing the motionless trees, Olga suddenly had an urge to be mean. She was watching Charles drinking, smoking, in the yellow shadowy light, and she was smiling with hate at this man, at the control of nerves, sex, and blood which he exercised over her. She was following him to hell. She will be beyond reach. Far below, hate did not have to be differentiated from love. It is possible that hate had always preceded love and we remain so aggressive because of it. We would not have to resist, to persist any longer;

we could let go, see ourselves as we are; we could let ourselves slide; we could leave the surface, go down to the bottom of ourselves and finally reach the depths of deception. To see ourselves face-to-face. No longer invent a man or a woman other than what we are; we were no longer immortal; we no longer had false ideals; we were mortal; we were no longer lovers; we were enemies; there was no longer a need to try pathologically to supplement the immeasurable void or space. Then, on earth, maybe another life, a resurrection, an atonement could begin; then, wearied of being in the lowest depths of inhumanity, we could catch a glimpse or shred of truth, and pick ourselves up inside and set out again toward only what is true . . . a god more real. . . .

"After me, you won't have any more illusions," Charles whispers.

When we reach the bottom of our being, do we still have what it takes to live? Do we still have enough air, enough light? Is it not too depressing? Too close to crime? Charles and Olga sat forlorn in the faint glow shed by the decay fossilizing the visions, the movements of a planet in distress, where men, women, victims of their solitude, were crashing. . . .

"Tell me that you love me," Olga demanded.

In the razor-sharp dusk, Charles's face was fractured by the play of light.

Olga was begging. "Take me in your arms. . . ."

He pushed her back, "This is not the right time. There's too much tension between us. Let's wait."

He was retreating, faithful to what tactical role, she was not sure; Charles wanted her to submit to the tyranny with which he was trying to control her; he wanted to play with the frightened flame he was creating in the eye of this woman in love. He was drowning in a decaying world. Reality was vanishing in the luminescence of lines and silhouettes, in the uncertainty that was cutting in two all that Olga and he were trying to recognize in the ramification, in the proliferation of the inner darkness, where, through propagation, through contamination, the human shadows were carrying on . . . God . . . God?

Olga . . . Olga. . . . Charles is right up against her; he is panting, caught up in a swirl of cosmic dust, of mineral particles, in this mud of memory where he is led by the red sludge which is dragged out to sea by the terrible flow, amid the waves of the high sea of love. . . .

"Olga. . . ."

From the depths of time when you were still Esther, when the sun was still at its zenith, I was five years younger than today; I loved you; it was not yet this semi-obscurity where I can barely see you, where I no longer know if I love you. You were resplendent. We were young. I wanted to live. The wind whipped your hair, red like an arctic fox;

in my hands, you shone like the snow. We had not slept all night. Our place was not this Parisian park, these cafés, it was the vastness of a windy beach; we were right at the beginning of ourselves; I was holding you in my arms; I was lost in your salty curls, in their taste of sea spray.

"I want you," Charles whispered to the American. He had set her down in the blue sludge, in the blue-colored puddles, between the blocks, the pebbles. The air was luminous and cold like a polar sea, as if we were miles from dry land. . . . We had eloped to this world of birds, fish, mussels, clams, winkles, where we were the only humans on a shore covered with crushed shells, under a sun specked with red where the dunes rippled like grass igloos. Desire returns to him. Charles wanders through this body of soft skin and odors, through the island in the distant bay, through Esther taken so far away where one dreams, to the edge of the ice floe, through the winter camps, through the spring camps, through June where the seals sun themselves on the ice, through Olga, to the north of reason, through the territories of a mad journey, at the very end of an icy, deserted heart where almost nothing is left in a secret that Charles haunts night and day through the stifling city where he takes Olga outside of herself but he finds its site again; he finds its lips, its mucus membranes, and it is almost softer, now, after death; it is almost softer in this other woman, in her hair as cozy as the down of the ducks which nested on the northeast shore of the bay, near the lakes full of fish where Esther would take Charles, to the north of love from which he never returned and where, in the pockets of icy running water left behind by spring, he sees the reflection of something like eyes, a dead sky. . . .

The red color of the clay from the great depths disappears as the night of the spirit increases, when along the way, like fat marine mammals, the monsters assemble in pale herds, when he still has the yearning to kill, when he is not yet free of the remorse that stifles his breath.

Charles, leaning toward Olga, breathes with difficulty and, as though he were trying to support his heart, places his hand on his right side in this migratory circuit, in this depopulation of the bay bordered with high hills of the imaginary to which is attached the ghostly village governed by a distant Federal Ministry of Northern Affairs. The summer he spent at Quaqtaq, his hunting, fishing expeditions, his nomadic memories do not render him sedentary, no longer integrate themselves to the North American reality that had bewitched him. . . .

He no longer knows who Olga is, who he is . . . where he is.

He can no longer communicate.

⌐15⌐

It is raining. The taxis are driving slowly over the pavement. Passers-by, sheltered by their umbrellas, are running. In the restaurant Place du Tertre, Olga is thinking about Charles, seated in front of her. Olga sees the lights of Paris shimmering outside, the Eiffel Tower in the distance. The more Olga is alive, alive with this tense man, the more Charles prefers absence to her. Barely born, life dies. The aching love for life, the aching desire for life, while this man is languishing. . . . To look at him, to look for him in his enigmatic face which might not be his and which, turned toward some unknown destination, despises the world and goes off toward an invisible star. . . .

Charles, later on, in the car, lightly brushes Olga with his lips and his tongue, "You're alive? Are you alive?"

Charles leaves lunar soil, devoid of light, only to go toward the colors of memory, the purples, the beiges, the greys of the roads snaking through mountain passes the color of lichen, rock, bark, inside Charles's lungs brought back to life when Esther would take him to pick irises, when Charles, near Esther, would breathe in the scents of spring, when he would escape from the desertification, from the petrification of his inner world.

Charles is having difficulty breathing.

He has sacrificed the bluishness of the infinite horizon, the river inlets in the bays and the estuaries, the shores of Two Mountain Lake, Green Island, the kingdom of brown agate and jasper where salmon, herring, trout, eel, beaver, bear, porcupine, scallops, crabs, smelt, sturgeon, bustard, teal, cod, lobster, halibut resided in the strawberry red, raspberry red, gooseberry red spaces of the blood's vigor which, mad with love, Charles would use to be united to his magical Esther, before the coming of the freeze and the first snows, in this man's flesh ready to sleep, ready to repress, at any price, the power of a desire tormented by cruelty, hate, fear. . . .

For him, love is a distant country, barely explored, where once he ventured to the farthest limits of the border that separates the earth from madness . . . beyond the pole of a planet where he dared go all the way to the north without being able to stop his forward movement, toward the extreme cold and night of muted despair, blind to life, which always attempts to hold us back.

Little by little Charles was going to become inured to the mental winter, to the swirls of interior snow that clot your blood; he had been afraid of reaching a state of total immobilization; his whole being had begun to operate in slow motion. Charles was curtailing his gestures, his movements. Experiencing an urgent need to feel secure, he had returned to Europe. But in this scriptwriting woman, this Olga Vassilieff, everything was brutally starting all over again. . . . Charles is traveling through impossible, remote zones where cold weather lasts longer than anywhere else; where there are still virgin forests. However much he tries to remain alone in his corner, to brood silently over his problems, he must set out again toward her; she is here, too alive, too present; she is calling him over there; try as he may to flee these swirls of burning snow, these nights blue with snow, they are in his blood; in his head, he hears the ghostly neighbors shoveling the raging snow in front of the house, the violent winds sweeping the province buried under a foot of snow fallen in just a matter of hours; he remembers the electrical failures, the power outages, the signs torn off, the television antennas broken, the plaster on the hospital wall ripped away by gale-force winds reaching eighty miles an hour, the helplessness of the snow-removal crew and Esther in the cloudy night, in this blue light of a northern winter reflected in the wide-open eyes of this woman, Olga, whom, with a desperate passion, Charles is, here in his dream, penetrating all the way to her soul, all the way to Esther, all the way to all these nights powdery with snow, in the country of solitude where storms forecasted by the weather reports would inter- rupt the lulls during which Charles and Esther, even at midnight, dared to go out, dared to walk on the slippery sidewalk. He would overhear snatches of conversations in the street, "Don't forget your snow pants or else you'll get cold snowshoeing. . . ." One winter, Charles and Esther had rented an overheated apartment in Montreal. Charles was not thinking about going all the way to Artabassa yet . . . always farther, with this woman. The roads in the east were closed to traffic; every morning the entrance to the house had to be cleared. The squalls persisted. Charles would stroll through the deserted English part of town. Esther would wait for him nice and warm in the bedroom of the rented apartment. She would listen to the radio announcing that the wind, outside the city, had flipped some trucks over. Charles, victim of a strange euphoria, would extend his strolls in the snow until dawn. Charles did not feel anything, did not see anything of the outside; he would walk through the cold of the streets as though he were inside this woman's skin more refined, more transparent than a fetus where a network of veins appears to be drawn on its surface. Charles was inside her, always inside her, her prisoner; he needed to walk, to get away from the bedroom which, after each embrace, the American, the black widow, the spider woman, infused with her charm, leaving Charles dazed; "I love the dead . . . I love the dead," repeated the vocalist whom Esther would tirelessly listen to singing "The Black Widow" . . . "I love the dead," *j'aime la mort* Charles would translate, humming these rhythms that sent shivers of excitement through him . . . "You criminal . . . you, go to hell . . ." Charles would continue, would improvise, "I drink blood and milk. I got no choice. I'm the devil. . . ."

Down what slope of sounds, of violence, of cries, and of silence was Esther dragging him? He would confuse her with the snowfalls, with Alice Cooper, with the desolation of the city in the night.

"Killer. . . . Yeah! yeah! killer!" screamed Alice Cooper in Charles's ears. . . . "Baby, you love the dead, you don't know what I say. . . ." Charles would have liked to cover his ears so that Esther's favorite record would not invade him. He would have liked to defend himself, to become this sea scorpion whose stingers, if it is disturbed, discharge a poison, but the black widow was wearing him down; even his desire for her was poisoned by the venom which she secreted amid explosions of light where she was this flame, this beauty against which Charles was throwing himself in the oral cavity of the monster whose tongue, like tentacles, would paralyze him with a bite for the whole night. I drink blood and milk; I got no choice, I'm the devil. . . . "Tell me . . . tell me . . . who I really am. . . ." No, in her arms, he no longer knew who he was, whether he was her. . . . Tell me . . . tell me who I really am. . . . He no longer knew if it was madness, if he was still himself. . . . And he would weep in the Plamondon and the Queen Mary neighborhoods, while Alice Cooper kept on singing "I never cry. . . . Open it up but don't you leave it alone and you know: I never cry . . . I never cry . . . and you know. . . . You know . . . why I never cry . . . why I disappear. . . . Yeah . . . *pour quoi je disparais.* . . . Yeah . . ."

Olga . . . the Parisian summer . . . the bench in Monceau Park; what does this man in love have left of life that he can give to this living woman? They both died in Artabassa, in America's north, five years ago. . . . Even if, fleetingly, Esther lives again suddenly in the seduction of an apparition, "Olga," Charles whispers, "I think I love you. . . ."

He repeats her name several times: Olga, Olga. Suddenly he loves her belly. Suddenly he loves her hips . . . suddenly he loves her mouth . . . yes, especially the mouth with the full lips. . . . But that is not her. . . . Where is he? Olga parts open under Charles's teeth. She moans. He is going down into this woman back from the grave; he loves women, any women, since they are always her, since they are never her, at the depths of fifteen feet where the natural light is very weak, making it difficult to bring up pictures of underwater life, to photograph the interior ocean, this black queen, the skeleton skull, the submerged scenery, the delirium where, holding his breath, the man in love had dived into the maze of arms and branches where Esther, too motherly, like a hidden river, poured forth her waters under areas of strong light and under earthly cloud banks, just north of himself, right where he felt capable of strangling, amid these impulses that suddenly come back to him, in a Parisian park. Olga is stretched out on the bench, under Charles, who is nibbling at her neck, holding her tight, "The last night . . .," he says in English.

"Why in English?" asks Olga, afraid and not knowing why.

"It was the last night. . . . My star. . . . My dead . . .," he repeats in English.

Avoid her. Avoid facing her. Charles is getting worse. He has lost control of the nightmare. Olga is too close to him. He is afraid of what he might do. He is going to confess. He has to speak, to bite, to bite harder, to squeeze this woman; the world is getting strange, hazy again. Charles feels his throat tighten. He gets up. His breathing is labored. He stares at her without recognizing her in the abrupt, winter metamorphosis of the park where his surge of love and desire just got blocked.

He hates her. He hates women. "Please," cried Esther. "Please. . . ." Who is he? A killer? A homosexual killer having surrendered to criminal urges? A wolfman? But he had adored her. . . .

One morning, in the kitchen, Esther had burst into tears, complaining that she was lonely. . . . How many months had he kept her depressed, passive, had he forsaken her before killing her? These women, sticky with viscera, nauseated him. It was always back to weewee and poopoo when it came to the body, always back to disgusting things; it was always necessary to rebuff the other, otherwise they would ask you to lick them; you would continuously soil yourself inside them; they were intolerable masses of organs. Sometimes I drink more but I never cry, you cannot break my heart of stone, believe me, Babe, my heart's a virgin, and you know, I never cry . . . Charles continued to hum to himself in English. Esther would listen to Alice Cooper while Charles indulged in alcohol, walling himself up in impotence, in the impossibility of loving. But he was furiously searching for the road to love. He wanted to love; he wanted to desire. He still wants to love; he still wants to desire. Olga might be his last chance. To love? What does it mean to love? Is it when our heart is mad with hatred and death? when we have killed? when we have wandered for too long through icy solitudes and have walked on the ice of frozen lakes as on a road and have searched all around, beyond the mountains, for a planet where life could be reborn, far from the too-real earth? What is madness?

Olga shivers. She looks at the hands, the long fingers, the fingers of a pianist. In spite of their elegance, Charles's hands can be frightening. Olga resents her own inability to turn back, to leave Charles. But in the summer, being alone is less bearable. Her bouts of insomnia are even more wearing, especially this particular summer, more beautiful, so much more beautiful than the others. . . . Olga realizes that to live without love, as she has done for all these years, is not living. . . . Olga asks herself the question of a lifetime: "What is life?" When is the body at its greatest intensity? What height of passion must one attain to be certain to have lived, even for a few moments, only a few moments out of a whole lifetime? amid all the waste of a life, when, even for just a few minutes, your skin, your nerves, your muscles, your electricity, your magnetism, your mind will have been focused so that sensibilities will function, suddenly free, complete, turning you into the kind of woman all women dream of becoming one day thanks to a man?

"Are you happy when you're with me?"

Does Olga know that in Charles's mind she is Esther?

Charles's hands are shaking. The hands of an alcoholic or of a neurotic? He forces a laugh. She is on her guard. Something is going to happen. She will have to escape in time. What is living? What is madness?

"I was visually drunk, I could not see anything in front of me. It was the first time in my life that I could stay almost a month looking in the distance, without a house or inhuman cities blocking my view. To be able to see this infinity, this distance, to the ends of the earth, to the ends of the sky. I have never experienced this . . . I could see the fields of snow . . . the sea of snow. Places, names, times, everything would be mixed up. I have tried to soundproof my head. I wanted everything to be white, padded in this house at the ends of the world. No one came to our house. I had peace and quiet. I did without everything. The seasons went faster than I.

"I work all day long the way a river free of obstructions flows. The current passes at the right place. It's a little as if I were trying to mix two opposite life urges in order to try to create a third one, a fourth one. I know that I write in an unnatural way. I write with a knife, with the cutting edge of a knife . . . gashing, cutting. . . ."

Olga has a chill; she pictures in her mind Charles taking life away. . . . The outlines of the paths in Monceau Park, all the way to the Boulevard Courcelles, disappear in the fog from which protrude the tops of the columns.

"Let's walk a little," says Olga. "I'm cold."

They get up, walk along the pathway that goes around the park. Charles scrutinizes the clumps of shrubs and flowers, the lawns, the banana tree, the little brook, the artificial cave, as though trying to reassure himself that no one is hiding. He inspects the park; he checks that the railings encircle him, that the monumental doors, in a little while, will close off access to the three avenues and the entrance at the boulevard.

"I don't feel well," says Olga. "I want to go home."

"It's this fog," says Charles. "Soon we won't be able to see six feet in front of us."

The summer is taking a turn for the worse. Olga is sullen. Something in Charles has caved in. She would like to hold him up, to whisper to him that she is here. . . . But he does not pay any attention to her. He is not with her. . . . She cannot make him happy. Yes, so, Olga wonders what life is, if she is living, if it would not be better for her to stop trying so desperately to live, when we can never manage to do it. . . .

'16'

Esther and Charles stumble into a discotheque painted entirely black. Single bodies. Single boys. Single girls. The smoke from the cigars and the cigarettes shrouds the pool table and a few players. The dancers on the floor float about weightlessly like astronauts walking on the moon. This rhythmic place shelters broken harmonies, repetitious sounds, machines, autoeroticism, shadows, sounds of machine guns or bombings, a whole generation of unemployed who play the guitar and beg in subway corridors. The music imitates the roar of rocket firings, shell explosions. The videotape players glow on the walls lighted like the instrument panel of a fighter plane. Masses for atheists, for the hopeless, for survivors, celebrated by this city of graffiti and garbage cans. Esther would accompany Charles in his drifting off where they liked to meet, drink, dance in the winter night, in this underground chorale of electronic voices. Around them, semi-humans, semirobots from the year 2000 or cherubs with vampire heads, hairy, beautiful, dressed in their outlandish style, were turning into zombies listening to siren whistles, to percussion in this interior design of rubble. All these stoned, alcoholic young people were imitating missiles, torpedo boats, the architecture of a fallout shelter, the aerial raids of the coming apocalypse. Charles, drowsy, would smoke. Esther, under the influence of urges intensified by this club located on the fourth floor of a skyscraper, would squirm on her stool. This alternative music exported to America from London made her dizzy.

Charles looks at Olga. The too-familiar Parisian imprisons him in this city that is too small, in this country that is too small, on this continent that is too small. . . . How can we enlarge the mental field diminished day by day by the necessity to adapt to reality? What can be done to rediscover the vastness of infinite emotions, to taste life as though tasting an exotic dish, as though savoring carrot or corn muffins for the first time, as if tasting cheddar, or pork chops served with apple sauce in the Ottawa restaurant near the Lord Higgins Hotel where Esther and Charles had a room? What can be done to recover the feeling of being among new surroundings again? What can be done to enlarge the earth? push the walls back? the bones of the skull? open the brain, give back to it the light that people no longer see? What can be done to overcome the meagerness of the black night where we are despondent as in a prison or psychiatric hospital cell?

What can be done to live again when we have killed as though we had committed suicide? How many miles do we need to go to catch another glimpse of the outside, its large cities, its bars, their basketsful of fries, the ice cubes in a glass of carbonated water, the packs of sugar and pasteurized cream for the coffee? After leaving Montreal, Charles and Esther had spent a week in Ontario before going on to Artabassa. What can be done to travel again across the emptiness of these ghostly three thousand five hundred miles? again to fly over the Saint Lawrence, then Newfoundland? when the beloved woman is no more than a corpse, than a souvenir? What can be done to enjoy comfort, luxury, when you are a pariah, when you have damned yourself, in one night, for all eternity? "What do you want?" "What do you drink?" When you hate yourself because you did not know how to love, because you have never learned how to love? "Are you happy?" "Yeah! we are happy. . . ." "OK boys!" Charles, snug near Esther in the Ottawa bar, each night had the impression of being inside a Christmas tree, inside the branches of a fir tree twinkling with multi-colored balls. The outside sounds were muffled by the upholstery, by the velvet of the chairs. Charles was reveling in, was savoring Esther's beauty. Time had stopped. Charles was hibernating in tranquillity, numb with the joy of being there with this woman for a few hours where shadows and reflections were warded off, where nothing in Charles any longer contradicted his need for Esther. . . .

"Hello!"

"Lovely. . . ."

The candles were burning, dark red, brown. Charles and Esther, apart from the others, could hear only the sighs of contentment, the yawns of the patrons, and were looking out the little window at the winter, the wet street, the melted snow, the last cars of the night. The bar was the color of placenta, mucous red rays, squares. The far end of the library was wallpapered with red and purple plaid fabric. A crown of holly, pine cones, and mistletoe was hung above the door like a painting.

"He's so natural. . . ."

The carpet was wine-colored. This bar, all reds and half-lights, was a little like the inside of a body. You felt like letting go, no longer fighting, no longer opposing someone, as though there were no more adversaries, as though there were only love. . . .

What is madness? It is this discharge which, all at once, ruptures harmony. It is pearl necklaces, crystal beads, earrings, pendants which unfold, multiply on a face split up into an infinity of faces that mock you, incite you, smile at you; he lacerates her, he takes over this beauty, he puts it on, he rips the skin. He backs up instead of going forward. He is going backwards. It is in backing up that he discovers his destiny. By returning to the beginning, by letting out little cries of pleasure, by disfiguring her, by amputating her because he is afraid suddenly, too afraid of her. . . .

Like Artemis, the sister with the golden sword, like the avenging archeress, like thoughts struggling against the invisible obstacle, Charles is fighting against Esther, against this haunting past, against this madness that keeps him away from any woman. The madman is cut off from himself. His reasoning is intermittent. The one occupying his insides drags Charles outside of his own body. Charles cannot, no more than before, hold back his other birth, his other sex, this murky part, this hell. Continuously he gives birth to a corpse with which he devours himself. He is going to be run through with holes. Any glance in his direction is hostile, seizes him, imprisons him. Charles struggles so as to leave nothing of the adversary intact. He must dismantle her, make her lose her mind. Thus he uses desire; he brings the other down to the level of an animal. He hears her honk like a goose. He clutches her, irritates her, vanquishes her with pleasure. He gets rid of the pursuer who was going to catch up with him and denounce him to himself. All he has left to do is flee, to become lost. Charles catches his breath, starts off again, even more determined, even more in a hurry to escape from the one who accuses him, from the one who betrays him, from life. . . . "You have gone beyond your powers and into hate," life tells him. However, he feels that he has never been so close to loving, to finding himself again. For this reason he must act more resolutely, faster. . . . He has run out of time. She disarms him. She is too hasty. She implores him with eyes that awaken pain. Who is she?

He is mad. . . . He is mad. He feels himself raving. He works late into the night against the savage beast, at the risk of making himself sicker. He never has a free moment anymore. She is here, once again. . . . She fixes her big eyes on him in an appeal for help. He uses force with her; he fights. He wants to survive this death wish. He wants to be free from it. He relies on pain for deliverance. There is never enough suffering. Sexuality is never sufficiently minimized; only physical ability counts in destroying oneself and in destroying the other. We only love to hate. We imagine life as dead. We kill or we commit suicide. As though she could die . . . as though we had enough hate inside us to tame this life as old as the universe. We fantasize reliving our wedding night. We marry hell, damnation, the fall into the abyss. Coitus devastates us. Charles felt like strangling, but even more than strangling, he felt like being strangled, like being this woman that he could still feel dying in his twitching fingers. He has stomach cramps. He is once again the dark mother giving birth, discharging. He wallows in obsession. He foams, bubbles in this flow of mad female debris. His voice changes, breaks. A demon straddles him. The voice of a female. He yelps in the woods, in the dark woods of rumor, "I love you." "You're so gorgeous, so nice," he shouts hoarsely in this scratchy voice of an old woman, in this crowd of voices of old women, in this repetition, in this rumination where the old woman, skin creased with lines, wraps her in spasms and in blood where he penetrates Olga with sadistic eyes, mad eyes.

"I love your face. . . ."

Charles frightens Olga. He transforms her into a thousand-year-old idol. He speaks an unknown language. He is the son of what goddess with a crumbling skeleton? Into what grave is he leading, is he putting this living woman in the place of a ghost?

The realm of the bony, toothless mother comes back to life. She was daughter to strange, unpronounceable names, Guthan, Archiwald, Maroald, Marulf, Agiulf, Brinnan, and reigned over mountains, forests, brooks, over barns whose noble queen she was, feisty with an untamable will, a warrior with the boiling temperament of a man. She was the bearded woman, the giant from the ancient north, the terrible one before everything capsized, was left to the ice, to the seals, to the bears in imaginary fallow lands where the son dreams of the aristocratic woman who raised him, passed on to him her values and, when death was about to snatch her away, bequeathed him courage and fierceness.

Esther or Olga could have been called Aude-Hilda, could have been of the Vandal-Gothic race like Charles's ancestor, fifteen centuries old, the ancient polytheistic northerner similar to the tattooed, colorful tribes that galloped from the east toward the west. . . . This unknown world was surfacing again in her barbaric language. There were piercing, disruptive and unusual noises, the onset of madness, a dialect of fear, with sounds that a scholar might have associated with the Frankish, the Gothic, the Germanic languages; she was shrill; she was screaming, "Charles! Charles!" And the well-mannered son had to obey his countess mother, "Yes, you wanted to speak to me, Mother?" She prevented him from plunging into himself. . . . He could no longer communicate with anyone. She was too present, like a loud attack, like these guttural names from the Ostrogoth, Visigoth, Vandal languages, Charles's Germanic roots, the onomatopoeia of this mad lineage. If it had not been for this unrestrained noise which she continuously made in him, he would have been calmer, but she was tyranizing him; she demanded that he respect her origins; within, he could feel continuous friction, spasms similar to the tires of Esther's car squealing on the snow, and the sound was getting louder, old Celtic, Roman, Germanic sounds like decibels reflected in the long golden braids of this mother-image, still tribal chief, echoing the sound waves of the past from which the present could not shield Charles's ears, the hoarse command never to forget, hurled past all women. . . . But he wanted to forget her; he wanted to kill her, to smash her skull; he wanted to be the son of a bitch, not of a queen; he suckled her night and day; he sucked her; he looked for her all over her flesh and placed his tongue under Olga's skin to the depths of her mucous membranes so she would shout louder, so she would enjoy even more completely this guilty, incestuous, forbidden enjoyment he was giving her, so blonde, as blonde as she was blonde and so white, as white as she was white; he was her son, her twin, her lover, his other self with a golden penis, and he made holes in women until he heard welling up from them this intensity of the tireless and daring female, a direct descendant of the reign of wind currents rustling among the high branches of the fir trees where the storm was incarnated in a female god with a man's head. Charles, because of this unbearably loud machine sound, could have lost his hearing. So he had ordered the din to cease. Esther was not to speak, nor Olga, nor any woman, nor anyone, nor the language itself, ever, was not to complain of the anger and the hatred which Charles directed at others during these self-mutations, during the history of blood and rage, the history of sadism, voyeurism, impotence, and vindictiveness as radiant, however, as love with which, suddenly, Olga was binding Charles to herself a little more each night. . . .

He would have liked to turn his back on her, make the life he was beginning to feel again take a different turn. He would question Olga. She was tired of answering. She could feel that he was not listening, that he did not understand. He was not interacting, he was distant; she could not communicate with him. He was inventing. He could hear only the voice. Only the sounds . . . a kind of music for him. . . . What Olga was saying was not important, did not need to make sense. The body was acting as a screen between Charles and her. He listened only to the shivers; he was submerged in this feminine resonance which issued from her sexuality, her belly, her warm saliva that he liked to sip from her lips while staring at her at times when they were talking. She was probably verbalizing distortions of the well-being that they both must have known a long time ago. The face, the smile, through Olga, continued to shine forth. Charles would have loved placing his head there, returning there to burrow, warm and protected, so he would never become a man again, so he could remain the son, only the son, the little boy whom these females with their disgusting appetites for sperm had always prevented him from being, between their fat knees, between their heavy thighs where he had felt like throwing up at times. . . . And, with his eyes, he was caressing Olga with the syllables, the whispers, the tenderness with which she was comforting him with her soft voice. He could hear himself saying, "I like feeling your hand on my brow, on my hair. . . ." He would let himself go. He was feverish; he could not breathe; when she whispered, it was as though these female lips were moving, slowly, all over his male body, as devoutly as though it were a corpse that could be resuscitated with such caring attention. As for her, she was thinking about the power of being alive that any woman dreams of giving to the man she loves, the man she wants to exalt, she wants to elevate, above her, above himself, to bring him closer to the living God. . . .

But when he was about to open up, he would once more withdraw within himself, near the red world where mystery hummed in Charles's blood; his head was swimming; Charles saw double; all women were nonbelievers, except this Olga, this Esther, the sacred ones, the two breasts on an enormous chest, and he was standing amid the racket, the uproar, amid the parts of himself which were always deserted like hiding places of which only he knew; he sought refuge in everything that he saw again as blurred, in the blonde Aude-Hilda with the scramasax, in this single-edged sword, this civilization of violence and murder which flowed through her veins and whose heir he was, detecting the bellowing of the fear generated within him by the cacophony produced by the nervous system, by the shrill tone of voice used by Esther or Olga, he could no longer tell which, to give orders, to holler, to impede conversation. Charles would have liked to tell Olga that he loved her. He tried to speak, but he felt full of hate. For thirty-six hours in a row, anger and despair isolated him, shaped in him imaginary trees and bushes like those in Monceau Park, as well as the sequoias of America, in this mad geography over which he would set out again, after each illusion of deliverance, when Olga had come so close, too close to him, that she moved him and that, to warm him, she threatened to cook his heart over a brisk fire. And in the country to which he would then escape alone, they would soon subsist on cormorants, penguins, ducks, lending their bird shapes to this man from the shadows who wished more than ever to emigrate to the north of himself, to leave again for the mental winter where everything is deep in darkness, where barely formed emotions freeze, cut down by the still and silent night. Hush . . . be still . . . allow the great void to spread over the doubt and the fear of being a human being, of belonging to the species where this woman was now looking at him too closely, where she was accusing him, where he could smell her breath on him, her eyes on him.

He would withdraw after having almost allowed himself to relent. Regressively, incestuously, he countered this postglacial woman with the successive glacial forward movements during the Quaternary era that engulfed regions of Europe, producing an ancient, mythical scenery. Olga would be lost in him as in uninhabited glaciers; in the inhospitable regions the travel would scratch her while Charles shifted between hope and despair, between the desire to live and the refusal to live. The mind of the murderer, divided between the real and the unreal, between two women, resembled a year of six months of days and six months of nights. He would dream of setting out on the road from west to east toward the cradle of his ancestors, as though going toward influxes coming from the Baltic Sea, from the islands of Bornholm and Gotland, in northern Europe where the habits of fog and cold, which had estranged him from others, took root in this distant man. Charles was reducing the outside to the inside, to a part of the inside. He was obsessed by the memory of his crime. It was too late; Olga could do nothing now. Neither could Paris, nor the summer. The traveler would set out again toward the wind, the storm, the sea, the rivers, the snow, the lakes, the forests, the mountains of yore, as though he were still a free man, with only the road before him. Part Oedipus, part Hamlet, he dreamed of changing continents, of crossing borders, of answering to customs agents' questions, "How many days are you planning to stay? Who are you visiting?" and of following the twists and turns of the map, going from south to north, toward the Great North, of seeing vegetable and mineral matter thicken, spread, encroach more and more on the social world, of seeing wild nature overrun civilization, of seeing more and more fir trees, fewer and fewer cities, fewer and fewer villages, fewer and fewer fields, fewer and fewer houses, more and more horizon, more and more clouds, more and more snow and ice. Once more he would have traveler's checks, Canadian dollars, and U.S. dollars. He would ride toward infinity; it would snow. The freeway would be deserted.

"Hey! Esther!"

"Hey! Charles!"

It is time for adventure. You depart without looking back. Desert vastness of the east. The east of the north. In search of your soul, you get lost along the shores, along interior images, along the random journey, in this limitless space; you depart, looking for an eternal season, for a winter which will never end. You will be cold there. You will become a hero of the loss of the self, of the loss of one's identity; you will shiver; you go where there are no more words, no more names; you no longer have a name; you are nothing anymore; your teeth chatter; you are just fighting against the strength and the speed of the wind and this burning pain caused by the snow as it stings your face as soon as you get out of the car, but you still go on, even on foot, but farther north, always farther north of these vast areas where nothing is born; you no longer have a past. You have left behind the urban hell, the smoky basements, the hugeness, the noise of rock music, traffic, swing, bottlenecks, jazz, the roar of airports, a sky streaked with planes that hover over as though they were overseeing this teeming metropolitan throng that evicted you from the earth because you have killed, and you go underground, into a gaping void, into the wound, into the forbidden zone where you are no longer yourself, you are no longer anyone, you no longer have parents, you no longer go anywhere; you no longer come from anywhere; you go on aimlessly, in this movie without a script, in our deserted heart, in this journey of psychic twists and turns that looks like a new world, but you have gone mad. Suffering has driven us mad. What kind of suffering? You do not know; you just suffer, slowly sinking deeper into it as our feet and legs sink back into the snow, on this road of disenchantment from which nothing alive will be brought back in our frozen body, nothing which will revive our soul abandoned by life's warmth as well as though by our mother. . . . Suddenly he looked at Esther with his cold eyes: "We don't need a motel, we'll sleep in the car."

"You want us to freeze to death?"

"I'll leave the heater on."

"You want to asphyxiate us?"

But he was pursued by authorities.

Rivière-au-Tonnerre, Wakefield, Matagami, Saint-Ferreol-les-Neiges, Mount Aurora, Koksoak River, Cap-Tourmente and this dense stretch of forest that the sun never penetrates, Opinaca, Cacouna, Prècieux-Sang, epic of snow, anger, and hatred; Sainte-Anne-des-Monts, Sainte-Esther-des-Monts, Sainte-Esther-des-Montagnes, Esther, virgin of the hills and the mountains, black Esther, Esther the Sphinx, Esther the color of islands, capes, lagoons, coves, archipelagos, Esther exposed to the north and west winds like a tender pink coast of flesh and mucous membranes. Esther with the strong swells, with the plateaus covered with red and purple grass, Esther with the great shore, Esther with the eagle nest, with the wilderness cove, her magnificent house overlooking the wind and the clouds. Esther with the rocky coasts where incest howled, howls still, Esther, before the crime, stony and denuded, Esther, the animal-mother to whom Charles devotes placental worship because this goddess was the placenta back in the memory of remote ages when she became united with the ancestral mountain to give birth to man, to Charles, the son of red sandstone, of sand block and of pebbles, the son of coagulated blood, the son of desire petrified before insatiable Esther who is never appeased, always thirsty for sperm, saliva, rapture, Esther the nymphomaniac, the carnivorous androphagist, the great wild goose, the wildfowl, the enormous mass of menstrual blood pouring straight down from a height of three hundred feet into these visceral landscapes where Charles's nerves were tied in knots, his muscles tetanized by the void, by this void never filled, this need of her, this inability to reach her. He did not know how to get across the multitude of dangerous river passes, how to go to the lakes speckled with gold, how to make his way through the brush gilded with frost, how to be the adventurer of the night and of death; all he had left were ancestral trails to connect the sparkling villages, her breasts, her belly, her vagina. The village of her two enormous breasts shining with milky snow, the village of her great belly where life resided. He did not know how to prolong within himself the presence of this land of the cold, glacial whiteness of her semi-obscurity, the nuances, the half-tones, the strangeness of these durations of a few seconds, the needless repetitions, the disconnected words where, from funereal tonality to funereal tonality, Esther's voice moved Charles amid the dusks of yesteryear, the obsessive dusks when he would be near her, seated in the kitchen listening to her, listening just to her voice shrouding the wind and the sound of the flowing river darkened by the setting sun. Charles, contemplative, received emanations from within which would return him to the fetal position, would make him curl up in this woman, in the incantatory function of the maternal voice which held him under its spell, communicated to him a muted echo of the vague grumbling from the outside world carried all the way to the top of the windy hill where Brendan had built the big house made of blue wood and white bricks for his wife, Esther the very beautiful, the most beautiful, Esther the musician with the aquatic accents of a little pond, of the basin, of the marsh where, bewitched, Charles went to snuggle up, to stagnate, to bathe in the mucus of the intoxicating female, in the secretion of these juices of joy which he caused to surge inside her, at night, embracing her, kissing the very beautiful, the most beautiful woman that Charles had ever seen, the woman of the black death. . . . Living not far from one of the great rivers of the world, bird-woman who went away one night, taking flight toward the fissures, the gaps, beyond the boreal light, beyond the thousands of foggy miles, to these tundras of the north, to these deserts of bushes and lichens, of fjords, of frozen waters in this frigid world, Charles's interior world to which Esther would never come back . . . where life was silent. . . .

Olga tries to tear him away from the void, to bring him closer to her: "I love you. I love you. Believe me. Believe it when I say that I love you."

She tries to revive him, to bring him back to sexuality, to sensuality, to desire. He did not believe her. She was lying. He would punish her. She was too beautiful, yes, too beautiful. Love is too beautiful. Charles would never be as beautiful as love. The only light Charles would ever be able to emit would be nothing more than this pale spark of hatred that cooled the air and poured through it like rapids of icy waters. . . .

'17'

It is dusk; Olga is walking in the park. Charles has not called. Olga has no more words for thinking, for writing. She no longer works. It is like a hemorrhage draining you of your blood. She is obsessed with Charles. Charles, more and more imaginary, less and less real. He refuses to go near her. He is up there, in the trees whose branches scratch Olga's eyes, Olga lost in this park, sad as in a cemetery whose lanes remind her of the absent man and the death, which, latent, uses up the female body. Olga believes only in life, wants only life. Each morning, she puts on her makeup, colors her cheeks, her eyelashes, her skin, her nails, the gestures of an Olga hoping to please. She picks out some lipstick, some rouge, some nail polish. She wants to convince this man that she is a woman, that the reds of her makeup are those of beautiful blood, of a sparkling stain of living blood. . . . The chemistry of the biological beauty of blood rushing to the skin's surface. In the evening, Olga's female body is blood circulation for contemplative Charles. Like those of a murderer tearing his victim apart, the voyeur's eyes focus on Olga's curves, she who is so alive, so warm, whose veins will be emptied, whose steaming warm stream swallowed, inhaled by Charles, if she opens up, if she squirts, if she agrees to be only corpuscles, only a bright redness, only an outpouring where there will appear some more-or-less distinct patterns sketching the corpuscle mosaic of some anterior life, a life mostly forgotten which, if it were not for this haunting red, would have become pale, colorless. But by sadistically, lovingly killing Esther, has not Charles rediscovered a fetal intimacy in these female inner parts like the womb, whose opening he can never feel at the tip of his penis, and which is the start of the long tunnel of life that he would like to travel in reverse so he could enter the belly that he cannot bring himself to leave as though he were not ready to be born? But they die, these mortal women, if we try to draw out from them a small piece of our origins with a knife as precise as a scalpel, and they do not heal up anymore; they do not stop flowing; we cannot sponge up anymore; we cannot transfuse anymore; misery assails you again with this liquid that is too red, too sticky, with this purple and bright red radiance that the mad lover was not satisfied just to admire by looking through, but one night went to Artabassa to drink straight from the severed artery of the one he did not know how to love with human feelings, but with animal feelings, with the pain of a baby brutally expelled from the gravid female. . . .

What torment then seizes the body, prevents it from being able to tell the difference between life and death, hate and love, a being, any being, from the first one, the only one, the being with the most feminine organs, in these maternal viscera, this pregnant motherhood? Oh! this subconscious and unforgettable impression that the dark viscera, which held us, has imprinted on all feelings, on all the emotions of our backward sexuality left lingering in instinct. Oh! the violence of human history, these generations that nothing will enlighten, that nothing will civilize, our remorseless savagery! This intermingling of the animal and the human in our species, beyond any light, beyond any conscience. . . . And this drive, oh! nothing but this drive to create and to destroy. . . .

Charles was picturing himself strangling Olga Vassilieff.

He was speaking in ever softer tones, in monosyllables, his face glum, his eyes downcast, his vegetative functions slower, diminished; everything in him was having difficulty in coming to light. . . . Olga was waiting. He was not yet alive but the moment would come when he would get free of the constraint, when breathing would begin, when he would stand, he would walk, he would puncture the mucus, the meconium, the amniotic fluid that was confining him, mummifying him in this fetal position, behind this membrane separating him from the others, and he would no longer be able to stand the lack of air; he would no longer be able to stand still being in touch with the organism of a ghost. He would discover the woman of flesh and blood, the true woman, her, Olga Vassilieff, fiercely determined to heal this man in a moribund state, and he would live, an extrauterine life. . . .

The air in the city, the air in the park, the air in Olga's apartment with the windows open onto the summer would enter Charles's lungs; Charles would come out of a dead woman to penetrate, finally, this live woman: Olga. And what was plugging up the openings would disappear, yes, and then, he would breathe vigorously; he would no longer revel in the putrefaction of a corpse; he would no longer be a puny man incapable of loving; he would grow. His desire would no longer be stillborn. Charles would go toward the woman to the end of the road with the arms, the vulva, and the long soft hair which he would become drunk smelling, smoothing, kissing; Olga was dreaming, aware of outside, the trees, the sweetness of the summer coming to an end. "It's so good to be alive," she would tell herself, but Charles, taciturn, stiff, went on obstinately refusing. Intuitively, Olga felt like shouting to him, "It's not too late. Even if you have done something irreparable. Since you're alive, since you're not dead, it's not too late. Dare! Begin! Come! Let's go! Come toward me. . . ." Olga continued to pray; granted there was no certainty of immortality, but here, in this fervor where life was always redeeming you, nothing was irreversible except death; and all this time that you were being spared by death belonged to life, to the reverence for triumphant life. As long as we were not dead, we still had a chance to help life go on, to conquer hatred, misery and madness; and if we cannot forgive evil, we must forgive life, this life which surpasses us and in which the wicked creature that we are is free to want to be better and to learn to do good, to reach the other, a trembling, liberating tenderness, in this same torment with which Charles knew he would horrify Olga if she were to discover what he was hiding from her, even if the motive for the murder was the disorder of Charles's mind which still prevented the pathetic wretch from seeing clearly. For dangerous individuals, isn't life no more than an inaccessible ideal? And don't they deserve something other than pain and punishment from it? Olga knew nothing of the need we can have to blame ourselves, pitilessly, and to set ourselves apart from others for whom we are nothing more than a menace. Nothing, she believed, deserves to lose the last resort which humanity gives to itself: charity. No, nothing. But the God that fixes what is broken, does he exist? The God that prevents our eyes from killing the stars when dawn appears, does he exist? The God of innocence, who excuses our incest, our sins, does he exist? The God for whom we are only irresponsible, infantile, silly creatures, does he exist? A God we can implore for grace, does he exist, in the sky where day and night regulate our evenings and our sleep led by the moon and the sun as by a prince of majesty and mercy, as by an optical testimony of light's celestial existence? A tangible God, a sensory God present before our eyes, our ears, our hands, does he exist?

The red snow, the endless snow roared in the constant winds that swept a city of icebergs risen from the coagulation of the ocean of decomposed blood in the sick brain that nothing any longer could cleanse of the memory of the cold region where Charles, without Esther, for a long time, wandered, mad, searching, over there, for the one whose heartbeat he no longer had. Oh! in the smile of this Olga, leaning over the sinner to help him, God, yes, does he exist? And she repeats to herself, closing her eyes so she will not see him anymore, "I love him. I love him."